Henry James OM (15 April 1843 – 28 February 1916) was an American-British author regarded as a key transitional figure between literary realism and literary modernism, and is considered by many to be among the greatest novelists in the English language. He was the son of Henry James Sr. and the brother of renowned philosopher and psychologist William James and diarist Alice James.

He is best known for a number of novels dealing with the social and marital interplay between émigré Americans, English people, and continental Europeans. Examples of such novels include The Portrait of a Lady, The Ambassadors, and The Wings of the Dove. His later works were increasingly experimental. In describing the internal states of mind and social dynamics of his characters, James often made use of a style in which ambiguous or contradictory motives and impressions were overlaid or juxtaposed in the discussion of a character's psyche.(Source: Wikipedia)

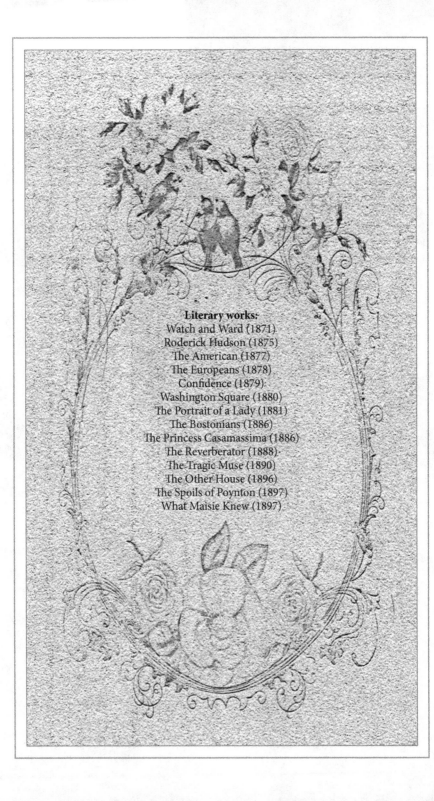

Literary works:
Watch and Ward (1871)
Roderick Hudson (1875)
The American (1877)
The Europeans (1878)
Confidence (1879)
Washington Square (1880)
The Portrait of a Lady (1881)
The Bostonians (1886)
The Princess Casamassima (1886)
The Reverberator (1888)
The Tragic Muse (1890)
The Other House (1896)
The Spoils of Poynton (1897)
What Maisie Knew (1897)

PRINCE CLASSICS

SIR DOMINICK FERRAND

HENRY JAMES

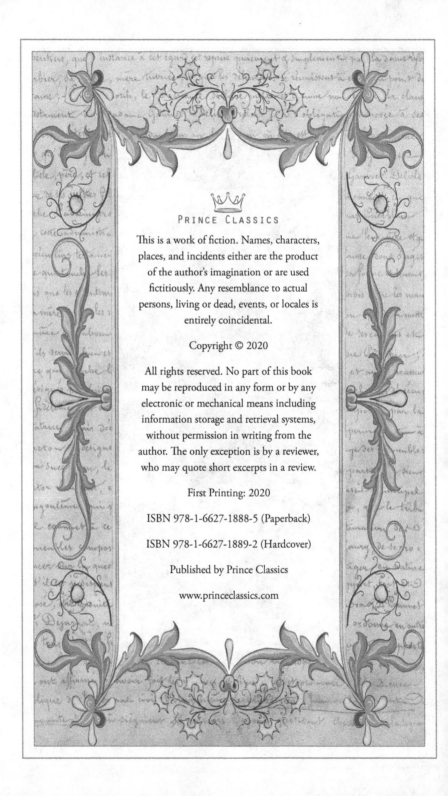

First Printing: 2020

ISBN 978-1-6627-1888-5 (Paperback)

ISBN 978-1-6627-1889-2 (Hardcover)

Published by Prince Classics

www.princeclassics.com

Contents

SIR
DOMINICK FERRAND

I.

"THERE are several objections to it, but I'll take it if you'll alter it," Mr. Locket's rather curt note had said; and there was no waste of words in the postscript in which he had added: "If you'll come in and see me, I'll show you what I mean." This communication had reached Jersey Villas by the first post, and Peter Baron had scarcely swallowed his leathery muffin before he got into motion to obey the editorial behest. He knew that such precipitation looked eager, and he had no desire to look eager—it was not in his interest; but how could he maintain a godlike calm, principled though he was in favour of it, the first time one of the great magazines had accepted, even with a cruel reservation, a specimen of his ardent young genius?

It was not till, like a child with a sea-shell at his ear, he began to be aware of the great roar of the "underground," that, in his third-class carriage, the cruelty of the reservation penetrated, with the taste of acrid smoke, to his inner sense. It was really degrading to be eager in the face of having to "alter." Peter Baron tried to figure to himself at that moment that he was not flying to betray the extremity of his need, but hurrying to fight for some of those passages of superior boldness which were exactly what the conductor of the "Promiscuous Review" would be sure to be down upon. He made believe—as if to the greasy fellow-passenger opposite—that he felt indignant; but he saw that to the small round eye of this still more downtrodden brother he represented selfish success. He would have liked to linger in the conception that he had been "approached" by the Promiscuous; but whatever might be thought in the office of that periodical of some of his flights of fancy, there was no want of vividness in his occasional suspicion that he passed there for a familiar bore. The only thing that was clearly flattering was the fact that the Promiscuous rarely published fiction. He should therefore be associated with a deviation from a solemn habit, and that would more than make up to him for a phrase in one of Mr. Locket's inexorable earlier notes, a phrase which still rankled, about his showing no symptom of the faculty really creative. "You don't seem able to keep a character together," this pitiless monitor had somewhere else remarked. Peter Baron, as he sat in his corner while the train stopped, considered, in the befogged gaslight, the bookstall standard of literature and asked himself whose character had fallen to pieces now. Tormenting indeed had always seemed to him such a fate as to have the creative head without the creative hand.

It should be mentioned, however, that before he started on his mission to Mr. Locket his attention had been briefly engaged by an incident occurring at Jersey Villas. On leaving the house (he lived at No. 3, the door of which stood open to a small front garden), he encountered the lady who, a week before, had taken possession of the rooms on the ground floor, the "parlours" of Mrs. Bundy's terminology. He had heard her, and from his window, two or three times, had even seen her pass in and out, and this observation had created in his mind a vague prejudice in her favour. Such a prejudice, it was true, had been subjected to a violent test; it had been fairly apparent that she had a light step, but it was still less to be overlooked that she had a cottage piano. She had furthermore a little boy and a very sweet voice, of which Peter Baron had caught the accent, not from her singing (for she only played), but from her gay admonitions to her child, whom she occasionally allowed to amuse himself—under restrictions very publicly enforced—in the tiny black patch which, as a forecourt to each house, was held, in the humble row, to be a feature. Jersey Villas stood in pairs, semi-detached, and Mrs. Ryves—such was the name under which the new lodger presented herself—had been admitted to the house as confessedly musical. Mrs. Bundy, the earnest proprietress of No. 3, who considered her "parlours" (they were a dozen feet square), even more attractive, if possible, than the second floor with which Baron had had to content himself—Mrs. Bundy, who reserved the drawing-room for a casual dressmaking business, had threshed out the subject of the new lodger in advance with our young man, reminding him that her affection for his own person was a proof that, other things being equal, she positively preferred tenants who were clever.

This was the case with Mrs. Ryves; she had satisfied Mrs. Bundy that she was not a simple strummer. Mrs. Bundy admitted to Peter Baron that, for herself, she had a weakness for a pretty tune, and Peter could honestly reply that his ear was equally sensitive. Everything would depend on the "touch" of their inmate. Mrs. Ryves's piano would blight his existence if her hand should prove heavy or her selections vulgar; but if she played agreeable things and played them in an agreeable way she would render him rather a service while he smoked the pipe of "form." Mrs. Bundy, who wanted to let her rooms, guaranteed on the part of the stranger a first-class talent, and Mrs. Ryves, who evidently knew thoroughly what she was about, had not falsified this somewhat rash prediction. She never played in the morning, which was Baron's working-time, and he found himself listening with pleasure at other hours to her discreet and melancholy strains. He really knew little about music, and the only criticism he would have made of Mrs. Ryves's conception of it was that she seemed devoted to the dismal. It was not, however, that these strains were not pleasant to him; they floated up, on the contrary, as a sort of conscious response to some of his broodings and doubts. Harmony, therefore, would have reigned supreme had it not been for the singularly bad taste of No. 4. Mrs. Ryves's piano was on the free side of the house and was regarded by Mrs. Bundy as open to no objection but that of their own gentleman, who was so reasonable. As much, however, could not be said of the gentleman of No. 4, who had not even Mr. Baron's excuse of being "littery" (he kept a bull-terrier and had five hats—the street could count them), and whom, if you had listened to Mrs. Bundy, you would have supposed to be divided from the obnoxious instrument by walls and corridors, obstacles and intervals, of massive structure and fabulous extent. This gentleman had taken up an attitude which had now passed into the phase of correspondence and compromise; but it was the opinion of the immediate neighbourhood that he had not a leg to stand upon, and on whatever subject the sentiment of Jersey Villas might have been vague, it was not so on the rights and the wrongs of landladies.

Mrs. Ryves's little boy was in the garden as Peter Baron issued from the house, and his mother appeared to have come out for a moment, bareheaded, to see that he was doing no harm. She was discussing with him the responsibility that he might incur by passing a piece of string round one of the iron palings and pretending he was in command of a "geegee"; but it happened that at the sight of the other lodger the child was seized with a finer perception of the drivable. He rushed at Baron with a flourish of the bridle, shouting, "Ou geegee!" in a manner productive of some refined embarrassment to his mother. Baron met his advance by mounting him on a shoulder and feigning to prance an instant, so that by the time this performance was over—it took but a few seconds—the young man felt introduced to Mrs. Ryves. Her smile struck him as charming, and such an impression shortens many steps. She said, "Oh, thank you—you mustn't let him worry you"; and then as, having put down the child and raised his hat, he was turning away, she added: "It's very good of you not to complain of my piano."

"I particularly enjoy it—you play beautifully," said Peter Baron.

"I have to play, you see—it's all I can do. But the people next door don't like it, though my room, you know, is not against their wall. Therefore I thank you for letting me tell them that you, in the house, don't find me a nuisance."

She looked gentle and bright as she spoke, and as the young man's eyes rested on her the tolerance for which she expressed herself indebted seemed to him the least indulgence she might count upon. But he only laughed and said "Oh, no, you're not a nuisance!" and felt more and more introduced.

The little boy, who was handsome, hereupon clamoured for another ride, and she took him up herself, to moderate his transports. She stood a moment with the child in her arms, and he put his fingers exuberantly into her hair, so that while she smiled at Baron she slowly, permittingly shook her head to get rid of them.

"If they really make a fuss I'm afraid I shall have to go," she went on.

"Oh, don't go!" Baron broke out, with a sudden expressiveness which made his voice, as it fell upon his ear, strike him as the voice of another. She gave a vague exclamation and, nodding slightly but not unsociably, passed back into the house. She had made an impression which remained till the other party to the conversation reached the railway-station, when it was superseded by the thought of his prospective discussion with Mr. Locket. This was a proof of the intensity of that interest.

12

The aftertaste of the later conference was also intense for Peter Baron, who quitted his editor with his manuscript under his arm. He had had the question out with Mr. Locket, and he was in a flutter which ought to have been a sense of triumph and which indeed at first he succeeded in regarding in this light. Mr. Locket had had to admit that there was an idea in his story, and that was a tribute which Baron was in a position to make the most of. But there was also a scene which scandalised the editorial conscience and which the young man had promised to rewrite. The idea that Mr. Locket had been so good as to disengage depended for clearness mainly on this scene; so it was easy to see his objection was perverse. This inference was probably a part of the joy in which Peter Baron walked as he carried home a contribution it pleased him to classify as accepted. He walked to work off his excitement and to think in what manner he should reconstruct. He went some distance without settling that point, and then, as it began to worry him, he looked vaguely into shop-windows for solutions and hints. Mr. Locket lived in the depths of Chelsea, in a little panelled, amiable house, and Baron took his way homeward along the King's Road. There was a new amusement for him, a fresher bustle, in a London walk in the morning; these were hours that he habitually spent at his table, in the awkward attitude engendered by the poor piece of furniture, one of the rickety features of Mrs. Bundy's second floor, which had to serve as his altar of literary sacrifice. If by exception he went out when the day was young he noticed that life seemed younger with it; there were livelier industries to profit by and shop-girls, often rosy, to look at; a different air was in the streets and a chaff of traffic for the observer of manners to catch. Above all, it was the time when poor Baron made his purchases, which were wholly of the wandering mind; his extravagances, for some mysterious reason, were all matutinal, and he had a foreknowledge that if ever he should ruin himself it would be well before noon. He felt lavish this morning, on the strength of what the Promiscuous would do for him; he had lost sight for the moment of what he should have to do for the Promiscuous. Before the old bookshops and printshops, the crowded panes of the curiosity-mongers and the desirable exhibitions of mahogany "done up," he used, by an innocent process, to commit luxurious follies. He refurnished Mrs. Bundy with a freedom that cost her nothing, and lost himself in pictures of a transfigured second floor.

On this particular occasion the King's Road proved almost unprecedentedly expensive, and indeed this occasion differed from most others in containing the germ of real danger. For once in a way he had a bad conscience—he felt himself tempted to pick his own pocket. He never saw a commodious writing-table, with elbow-room and drawers and a fair expanse of leather stamped neatly at the edge with gilt, without being freshly reminded of Mrs. Bundy's dilapidations. There were several such tables in the King's Road—they seemed indeed particularly numerous today. Peter Baron glanced at them all through the fronts of the shops, but there was one that detained him in supreme contemplation. There was a fine assurance about it which seemed a guarantee of masterpieces; but when at last he went in and, just to help himself on his way, asked the impossible price, the sum mentioned by the voluble vendor mocked at him even more than he had feared. It was far too expensive, as he hinted, and he was on the point of completing his comedy by a pensive retreat when the shopman bespoke his attention for another article of the same general character, which he described as remarkably cheap for what it was. It was an old piece, from a sale in the country, and it had been in stock some time; but it had got pushed out of sight in one of the upper rooms—they contained such a wilderness of treasures—and happened to have but just come to light. Peter suffered himself to be conducted into an interminable dusky rear, where he presently found himself bending over one of those square substantial desks of old mahogany, raised, with the aid of front legs, on a sort of retreating pedestal which is fitted with small drawers, contracted conveniences known immemorially to the knowing as davenports. This specimen had visibly seen service, but it had an old-time solidity and to Peter Baron it unexpectedly appealed.

He would have said in advance that such an article was exactly what he didn't want, but as the shopman pushed up a chair for him and he sat down with his elbows on the gentle slope of the large, firm lid, he felt that such a basis for literature would be half the battle. He raised the lid and looked lovingly into the deep interior; he sat ominously silent while his companion dropped the striking words: "Now that's an article I personally covet!" Then when the man mentioned the ridiculous price (they were literally giving it away), he reflected on the economy of having a literary altar on which one could really kindle a fire. A davenport was a compromise, but what was all life but a compromise? He could beat down the dealer, and at Mrs. Bundy's he had to write on an insincere card-table. After he had sat for a minute with his nose in the friendly desk he had a queer impression that it might tell him a secret or two—one of the secrets of form, one of the sacrificial mysteries— though no doubt its career had been literary only in the sense of its helping some old lady to write invitations to dull dinners. There was a strange, faint odour in the receptacle, as if fragrant, hallowed things had once been put away there. When he took his head out of it he said to the shopman: "I don't mind meeting you halfway." He had been told by knowing people that that was the right thing. He felt rather vulgar, but the davenport arrived that evening at Jersey Villas.

II.

"I DARESAY it will be all right; he seems quiet now," said the poor lady of the "parlours" a few days later, in reference to their litigious neighbour and the precarious piano. The two lodgers had grown regularly acquainted, and the piano had had much to do with it. Just as this instrument served, with the gentleman at No. 4, as a theme for discussion, so between Peter Baron and the lady of the parlours it had become a basis of peculiar agreement, a topic, at any rate, of conversation frequently renewed. Mrs. Ryves was so prepossessing that Peter was sure that even if they had not had the piano he would have found something else to thresh out with her. Fortunately however they did have it, and he, at least, made the most of it, knowing more now about his new friend, who when, widowed and fatigued, she held her beautiful child in her arms, looked dimly like a modern Madonna. Mrs. Bundy, as a letter of furnished lodgings, was characterised in general by a familiar domestic severity in respect to picturesque young women, but she had the highest confidence in Mrs. Ryves. She was luminous about her being a lady, and a lady who could bring Mrs. Bundy back to a gratified recognition of one of those manifestations of mind for which she had an independent esteem. She was professional, but Jersey Villas could be proud of a profession that didn't happen to be the wrong one—they had seen something of that. Mrs. Ryves had a hundred a year (Baron wondered how Mrs. Bundy knew this; he thought it unlikely Mrs. Ryves had told her), and for the rest she depended on her lovely music. Baron judged that her music, even though lovely, was a frail dependence; it would hardly help to fill a concert-room, and he asked himself at first whether she played country-dances at children's parties or gave lessons to young ladies who studied above their station.

Very soon, indeed, he was sufficiently enlightened; it all went fast, for the little boy had been almost as great a help as the piano. Sidney haunted the doorstep of No. 3 he was eminently sociable, and had established independent relations with Peter, a frequent feature of which was an adventurous visit, upstairs, to picture books criticised for not being *all* geegees and walking sticks happily more conformable. The young man's window, too, looked out on their acquaintance; through a starched muslin curtain it kept his neighbour before him, made him almost more aware of her comings and goings than he felt he had a right to be. He was capable of a shyness of curiosity about her and of dumb little delicacies of consideration. She did give a few lessons; they were essentially local, and he ended by knowing more or less what she went out for and what she came in from. She had almost no visitors, only a decent old lady or two, and, every day, poor dingy Miss Teagle, who was also ancient and who came humbly enough to governess the infant of the parlours. Peter Baron's window had always, to his sense, looked out on a good deal of life, and one of the things it had most shown him was that there is nobody so bereft of joy as not to be able to command for twopence the services of somebody less joyous. Mrs. Ryves was a struggler (Baron scarcely liked to think of it), but she occupied a pinnacle for Miss Teagle, who had lived on—and from a noble nursery—into a period of diplomas and humiliation.

Mrs. Ryves sometimes went out, like Baron himself, with manuscripts under her arm, and, still more like Baron, she almost always came back with them. Her vain approaches were to the music-sellers; she tried to compose— to produce songs that would make a hit. A successful song was an income, she confided to Peter one of the first times he took Sidney, blasé and drowsy, back to his mother. It was not on one of these occasions, but once when he had come in on no better pretext than that of simply wanting to (she had after all virtually invited him), that she mentioned how only one song in a thousand was successful and that the terrible difficulty was in getting the right words. This rightness was just a vulgar "fluke"—there were lots of words really clever that were of no use at all. Peter said, laughing, that he supposed any words he should try to produce would be sure to be too clever; yet only three weeks after his first encounter with Mrs. Ryves he sat at his delightful davenport (well aware that he had duties more pressing), trying to string together rhymes idiotic enough to make his neighbour's fortune. He was satisfied of the fineness of her musical gift—it had the touching note. The touching note was in her person as well.

17

The davenport was delightful, after six months of its tottering predecessor, and such a re-enforcement to the young man's style was not impaired by his sense of something lawless in the way it had been gained. He had made the purchase in anticipation of the money he expected from Mr. Locket, but Mr. Locket's liberality was to depend on the ingenuity of his contributor, who now found himself confronted with the consequence of a frivolous optimism. The fruit of his labour presented, as he stared at it with his elbows on his desk, an aspect uncompromising and incorruptible. It seemed to look up at him reproachfully and to say, with its essential finish: "How could you promise anything so base; how could you pass your word to mutilate and dishonour me?" The alterations demanded by Mr. Locket were impossible; the concessions to the platitude of his conception of the public mind were degrading. The public mind!—as if the public *had* a mind, or any principle of perception more discoverable than the stare of huddled sheep! Peter Baron felt that it concerned him to determine if he were only not clever enough or if he were simply not abject enough to rewrite his story. He might in truth have had less pride if he had had more skill, and more discretion if he had had more practice. Humility, in the profession of letters, was half of practice, and resignation was half of success. Poor Peter actually flushed with pain as he recognised that this was not success, the production of gelid prose which his editor could do nothing with on the one side and he himself could do nothing with on the other. The truth about his luckless tale was now the more bitter from his having managed, for some days, to taste it as sweet.

As he sat there, baffled and sombre, biting his pen and wondering what was meant by the "rewards" of literature, he generally ended by tossing away the composition deflowered by Mr. Locket and trying his hand at the sort of twaddle that Mrs. Ryves might be able to set to music. Success in these experiments wouldn't be a reward of literature, but it might very well become a labour of love. The experiments would be pleasant enough for him if they were pleasant for his inscrutable neighbour. That was the way he thought of her now, for he had learned enough about her, little by little, to guess how much there was still to learn. To spend his mornings over cheap rhymes for her was certainly to shirk the immediate question; but there were hours when he judged this question to be altogether too arduous, reflecting that he might quite as well perish by the sword as by famine. Besides, he did meet it obliquely when he considered that he shouldn't be an utter failure if he were to produce some songs to which Mrs. Ryves's accompaniments would give a circulation. He had not ventured to show her anything yet, but one morning, at a moment when her little boy was in his room, it seemed to him that, by an inspiration, he had arrived at the happy middle course (it was an art by itself), between sound and sense. If the sense was not confused it was because the sound was so familiar.

He had said to the child, to whom he had sacrificed barley-sugar (it had no attraction for his own lips, yet in these days there was always some of it about), he had confided to the small Sidney that if he would wait a little he should be intrusted with something nice to take down to his parent. Sidney had absorbing occupation and, while Peter copied off the song in a pretty hand, roamed, gurgling and sticky, about the room. In this manner he lurched like a little toper into the rear of the davenport, which stood a few steps out from the recess of the window, and, as he was fond of beating time to his intensest joys, began to bang on the surface of it with a paper-knife which at that spot had chanced to fall upon the floor. At the moment Sidney committed this violence his kind friend had happened to raise the lid of the desk and, with his head beneath it, was rummaging among a mass of papers for a proper envelope. "I say, I say, my boy!" he exclaimed, solicitous for the ancient glaze of his most cherished possession. Sidney paused an instant; then, while Peter still hunted for the envelope, he administered another, and this time a distinctly disobedient, rap. Peter heard it from within and was struck with its oddity of sound—so much so that, leaving the child for a moment under a demoralising impression of impunity, he waited with quick curiosity for a repetition of the stroke. It came of course immediately, and then the young man, who had at the same instant found his envelope and ejaculated "Hallo, this thing has a false back!" jumped up and secured his visitor, whom with his left arm he held in durance on his knee while with his free hand he addressed the missive to Mrs. Ryves.

As Sidney was fond of errands he was easily got rid of, and after he had gone Baron stood a moment at the window chinking pennies and keys in pockets and wondering if the charming composer would think his song as good, or in other words as bad, as he thought it. His eyes as he turned away fell on the wooden back of the davenport, where, to his regret, the traces of Sidney's assault were visible in three or four ugly scratches. "Confound the little brute!" he exclaimed, feeling as if an altar had been desecrated. He was reminded, however, of the observation this outrage had led him to make, and, for further assurance, he knocked on the wood with his knuckle. It sounded from that position commonplace enough, but his suspicion was strongly confirmed when, again standing beside the desk, he put his head beneath the lifted lid and gave ear while with an extended arm he tapped sharply in the same place. The back was distinctly hollow; there was a space between the inner and the outer pieces (he could measure it), so wide that he was a fool not to have noticed it before. The depth of the receptacle from front to rear was so great that it could sacrifice a certain quantity of room without detection. The sacrifice could of course only be for a purpose, and the purpose could only be the creation of a secret compartment. Peter Baron was still boy enough to be thrilled by the idea of such a feature, the more so as every indication of it had been cleverly concealed. The people at the shop had never noticed it, else they would have called his attention to it as an enhancement of value. His legendary lore instructed him that where there was a hiding-place there was always a hidden spring, and he pried and pressed and fumbled in an eager search for the sensitive spot. The article was really a wonder of neat construction; everything fitted with a closeness that completely saved appearances.

It took Baron some minutes to pursue his inquiry, during which he reflected that the people of the shop were not such fools after all. They had admitted moreover that they had accidentally neglected this relic of gentility— it had been overlooked in the multiplicity of their treasures. He now recalled that the man had wanted to polish it up before sending it home, and that, satisfied for his own part with its honourable appearance and averse in general to shiny furniture, he had in his impatience declined to wait for such an operation, so that the object had left the place for Jersey Villas, carrying presumably its secret with it, two or three hours after his visit. This secret it seemed indeed capable of keeping; there was an absurdity in being baffled, but Peter couldn't find the spring. He thumped and sounded, he listened and measured again; he inspected every joint and crevice, with the effect of becoming surer still of the existence of a chamber and of making up his mind that his davenport was a rarity. Not only was there a compartment between the two backs, but there was distinctly something *in* the compartment! Perhaps it was a lost manuscript—a nice, safe, old-fashioned story that Mr. Locket wouldn't object to. Peter returned to the charge, for it had occurred to him that he had perhaps not sufficiently visited the small drawers, of which, in two vertical rows, there were six in number, of different sizes, inserted sideways into that portion of the structure which formed part of the support of the desk. He took them out again and examined more minutely the condition of their sockets, with the happy result of discovering at last, in the place into which the third on the left-hand row was fitted, a small sliding panel. Behind the panel was a spring, like a flat button, which yielded with a click when he pressed it and which instantly produced a loosening of one of the pieces of the shelf forming the highest part of the davenport—pieces adjusted to each other with the most deceptive closeness.

This particular piece proved to be, in its turn, a sliding panel, which, when pushed, revealed the existence of a smaller receptacle, a narrow, oblong box, in the false back. Its capacity was limited, but if it couldn't hold many things it might hold precious ones. Baron, in presence of the ingenuity with which it had been dissimulated, immediately felt that, but for the odd chance of little Sidney Ryves's having hammered on the outside at the moment he himself happened to have his head in the desk, he might have remained for years without suspicion of it. This apparently would have been a loss, for he had been right in guessing that the chamber was not empty. It contained objects which, whether precious or not, had at any rate been worth somebody's hiding. These objects were a collection of small flat parcels, of the shape of packets of letters, wrapped in white paper and neatly sealed. The seals, mechanically figured, bore the impress neither of arms nor of initials; the paper looked old—it had turned faintly sallow; the packets might have been there for ages. Baron counted them—there were nine in all, of different sizes; he turned them over and over, felt them curiously and snuffed in their vague, musty smell, which affected him with the melancholy of some smothered

21

human accent. The little bundles were neither named nor numbered—there was not a word of writing on any of the covers; but they plainly contained old letters, sorted and matched according to dates or to authorship. They told some old, dead story—they were the ashes of fires burned out.

As Peter Baron held his discoveries successively in his hands he became conscious of a queer emotion which was not altogether elation and yet was still less pure pain. He had made a find, but it somehow added to his responsibility; he was in the presence of something interesting, but (in a manner he couldn't have defined) this circumstance suddenly constituted a danger. It was the perception of the danger, for instance, which caused to remain in abeyance any impulse he might have felt to break one of the seals. He looked at them all narrowly, but he was careful not to loosen them, and he wondered uncomfortably whether the contents of the secret compartment would be held in equity to be the property of the people in the King's Road. He had given money for the davenport, but had he given money for these buried papers? He paid by a growing consciousness that a nameless chill had stolen into the air the penalty, which he had many a time paid before, of being made of sensitive stuff. It was as if an occasion had insidiously arisen for a sacrifice—a sacrifice for the sake of a fine superstition, something like honour or kindness or justice, something indeed perhaps even finer still—a difficult deciphering of duty, an impossible tantalising wisdom. Standing there before his ambiguous treasure and losing himself for the moment in the sense of a dawning complication, he was startled by a light, quick tap at the door of his sitting-room. Instinctively, before answering, he listened an instant—he was in the attitude of a miser surprised while counting his hoard. Then he answered "One moment, please!" and slipped the little heap of packets into the biggest of the drawers of the davenport, which happened to be open. The aperture of the false back was still gaping, and he had not time to work back the spring. He hastily laid a big book over the place and then went and opened his door.

It offered him a sight none the less agreeable for being unexpected—the graceful and agitated figure of Mrs. Ryves. Her agitation was so visible that he thought at first that something dreadful had happened to her child—

that she had rushed up to ask for help, to beg him to go for the doctor. Then he perceived that it was probably connected with the desperate verses he had transmitted to her a quarter of an hour before; for she had his open manuscript in one hand and was nervously pulling it about with the other. She looked frightened and pretty, and if, in invading the privacy of a fellow-lodger, she had been guilty of a departure from rigid custom, she was at least conscious of the enormity of the step and incapable of treating it with levity. The levity was for Peter Baron, who endeavoured, however, to clothe his familiarity with respect, pushing forward the seat of honour and repeating that he rejoiced in such a visit. The visitor came in, leaving the door ajar, and after a minute during which, to help her, he charged her with the purpose of telling him that he ought to be ashamed to send her down such rubbish, she recovered herself sufficiently to stammer out that his song was exactly what she had been looking for and that after reading it she had been seized with an extraordinary, irresistible impulse—that of thanking him for it in person and without delay.

"It was the impulse of a kind nature," he said, "and I can't tell you what pleasure you give me."

She declined to sit down, and evidently wished to appear to have come but for a few seconds. She looked confusedly at the place in which she found herself, and when her eyes met his own they struck him as anxious and appealing. She was evidently not thinking of his song, though she said three or four times over that it was beautiful. "Well, I only wanted you to know, and now I must go," she added; but on his hearthrug she lingered with such an odd helplessness that he felt almost sorry for her.

"Perhaps I can improve it if you find it doesn't go," said Baron. "I'm so delighted to do anything for you I can."

"There may be a word or two that might be changed," she answered, rather absently. "I shall have to think it over, to live with it a little. But I like it, and that's all I wanted to say."

"Charming of you. I'm not a bit busy," said Baron.

Again she looked at him with a troubled intensity, then suddenly she demanded: "Is there anything the matter with you?"

"The matter with me?"

"I mean like being ill or worried. I wondered if there might be; I had a sudden fancy; and that, I think, is really why I came up."

"There isn't, indeed; I'm all right. But your sudden fancies are inspirations."

"It's absurd. You must excuse me. Good-by!" said Mrs. Ryves.

"What are the words you want changed?" Baron asked.

"I don't want any—if you're all right. Good-by," his visitor repeated, fixing her eyes an instant on an object on his desk that had caught them. His own glanced in the same direction and he saw that in his hurry to shuffle away the packets found in the davenport he had overlooked one of them, which lay with its seals exposed. For an instant he felt found out, as if he had been concerned in something to be ashamed of, and it was only his quick second thought that told him how little the incident of which the packet was a sequel was an affair of Mrs. Ryves's. Her conscious eyes came back to his as if they were sounding them, and suddenly this instinct of keeping his discovery to himself was succeeded by a really startled inference that, with the rarest alertness, she had guessed something and that her guess (it seemed almost supernatural), had been her real motive. Some secret sympathy had made her vibrate—had touched her with the knowledge that he had brought something to light. After an instant he saw that she also divined the very reflection he was then making, and this gave him a lively desire, a grateful, happy desire, to appear to have nothing to conceal. For herself, it determined her still more to put an end to her momentary visit. But before she had passed to the door he exclaimed: "All right? How can a fellow be anything else who has just had such a find?"

She paused at this, still looking earnest and asking: "What have you found?"

"Some ancient family papers, in a secret compartment of my writing-table." And he took up the packet he had left out, holding it before her eyes. "A lot of other things like that."

"What are they?" murmured Mrs. Ryves.

"I haven't the least idea. They're sealed."

"You haven't broken the seals?" She had come further back.

"I haven't had time; it only happened ten minutes ago."

"I knew it," said Mrs. Ryves, more gaily now.

"What did you know?"

"That you were in some predicament."

"You're extraordinary. I never heard of anything so miraculous; down two flights of stairs."

"*Are* you in a quandary?" the visitor asked.

"Yes, about giving them back." Peter Baron stood smiling at her and rapping his packet on the palm of his hand. "What do you advise?"

She herself smiled now, with her eyes on the sealed parcel. "Back to whom?"

"The man of whom I bought the table."

"Ah then, they're not from *your* family?"

"No indeed, the piece of furniture in which they were hidden is not an ancestral possession. I bought it at second hand—you see it's old—the other day in the King's Road. Obviously the man who sold it to me sold me more than he meant; he had no idea (from his own point of view it was stupid of him), that there was a hidden chamber or that mysterious documents were buried there. Ought I to go and tell him? It's rather a nice question."

"Are the papers of value?" Mrs. Ryves inquired.

"I haven't the least idea. But I can ascertain by breaking a seal."

"Don't!" said Mrs. Ryves, with much expression. She looked grave again.

"It's rather tantalising—it's a bit of a problem," Baron went on, turning his packet over.

Mrs. Ryves hesitated. "Will you show me what you have in your hand?"

He gave her the packet, and she looked at it and held it for an instant to her nose. "It has a queer, charming old fragrance," he said.

"Charming? It's horrid." She handed him back the packet, saying again more emphatically "Don't!"

"Don't break a seal?"

"Don't give back the papers."

"Is it honest to keep them?"

"Certainly. They're yours as much as the people's of the shop. They were in the hidden chamber when the table came to the shop, and the people had every opportunity to find them out. They didn't—therefore let them take the consequences."

Peter Baron reflected, diverted by her intensity. She was pale, with eyes almost ardent. "The table had been in the place for years."

"That proves the things haven't been missed."

"Let me show you how they were concealed," he rejoined; and he exhibited the ingenious recess and the working of the curious spring. She was greatly interested, she grew excited and became familiar; she appealed to him again not to do anything so foolish as to give up the papers, the rest of which, in their little blank, impenetrable covers, he placed in a row before her. "They might be traced—their history, their ownership," he argued; to which she replied that this was exactly why he ought to be quiet. He declared that women had not the smallest sense of honour, and she retorted that at any rate they have other perceptions more delicate than those of men. He admitted

26

that the papers might be rubbish, and she conceded that nothing was more probable; yet when he offered to settle the point off-hand she caught him by the wrist, acknowledging that, absurd as it was, she was nervous. Finally she put the whole thing on the ground of his just doing her a favour. She asked him to retain the papers, to be silent about them, simply because it would please her. That would be reason enough. Baron's acquaintance, his agreeable relations with her, advanced many steps in the treatment of this question; an element of friendly candour made its way into their discussion of it.

"I can't make out why it matters to you, one way or the other, nor why you should think it worth talking about," the young man reasoned.

"Neither can I. It's just a whim."

"Certainly, if it will give you any pleasure, I'll say nothing at the shop."

"That's charming of you, and I'm very grateful. I see now that this was why the spirit moved me to come up—to save them," Mrs. Ryves went on. She added, moving away, that now she had saved them she must really go.

"To save them for what, if I mayn't break the seals?" Baron asked.

"I don't know—for a generous sacrifice."

"Why should it be generous? What's at stake?" Peter demanded, leaning against the doorpost as she stood on the landing.

"I don't know what, but I feel as if something or other were in peril. Burn them up!" she exclaimed with shining eyes.

"Ah, you ask too much—I'm so curious about them!"

"Well, I won't ask more than I ought, and I'm much obliged to you for your promise to be quiet. I trust to your discretion. Good-by."

"You ought to *reward* my discretion," said Baron, coming out to the landing.

She had partly descended the staircase and she stopped, leaning against the baluster and smiling up at him. "Surely you've had your reward in the honour of my visit."

"That's delightful as far as it goes. But what will you do for me if I burn the papers?"

Mrs. Ryves considered a moment. "Burn them first and you'll see!"

On this she went rapidly downstairs, and Baron, to whom the answer appeared inadequate and the proposition indeed in that form grossly unfair, returned to his room. The vivacity of her interest in a question in which she had discoverably nothing at stake mystified, amused and, in addition, irresistibly charmed him. She was delicate, imaginative, inflammable, quick to feel, quick to act. He didn't complain of it, it was the way he liked women to be; but he was not impelled for the hour to commit the sealed packets to the flames. He dropped them again into their secret well, and after that he went out. He felt restless and excited; another day was lost for work—the dreadful job to be performed for Mr. Locket was still further off.

III.

TEN days after Mrs. Ryves's visit he paid by appointment another call on the editor of the Promiscuous. He found him in the little wainscoted Chelsea house, which had to Peter's sense the smoky brownness of an old pipebowl, surrounded with all the emblems of his office—a litter of papers, a hedge of encyclopædias, a photographic gallery of popular contributors—and he promised at first to consume very few of the moments for which so many claims competed. It was Mr. Locket himself however who presently made the interview spacious, gave it air after discovering that poor Baron had come to tell him something more interesting than that he couldn't after all patch up his tale. Peter had begun with this, had intimated respectfully that it was a case in which both practice and principle rebelled, and then, perceiving how little Mr. Locket was affected by his audacity, had felt weak and slightly silly, left with his heroism on his hands. He had armed himself for a struggle, but the Promiscuous didn't even protest, and there would have been nothing for him but to go away with the prospect of never coming again had he not chanced to say abruptly, irrelevantly, as he got up from his chair:

"Do you happen to be at all interested in Sir Dominick Ferrand?"

Mr. Locket, who had also got up, looked over his glasses. "The late Sir Dominick?"

"The only one; you know the family's extinct."

Mr. Locket shot his young friend another sharp glance, a silent retort to the glibness of this information. "Very extinct indeed. I'm afraid the subject today would scarcely be regarded as attractive."

"Are you very sure?" Baron asked.

Mr. Locket leaned forward a little, with his fingertips on his table, in the attitude of giving permission to retire. "I might consider the question in a special connection." He was silent a minute, in a way that relegated poor Peter to the general; but meeting the young man's eyes again he asked: "Are you—a—thinking of proposing an article upon him?"

"Not exactly proposing it—because I don't yet quite see my way; but the idea rather appeals to me."

Mr. Locket emitted the safe assertion that this eminent statesman had been a striking figure in his day; then he added: "Have you been studying him?"

"I've been dipping into him."

"I'm afraid he's scarcely a question of the hour," said Mr. Locket, shuffling papers together.

"I think I could make him one," Peter Baron declared.

Mr. Locket stared again; he was unable to repress an unattenuated "You?"

"I have some new material," said the young man, colouring a little. "That often freshens up an old story."

"It buries it sometimes. It's often only another tombstone."

"That depends upon what it is. However," Peter added, "the documents I speak of would be a crushing monument."

Mr. Locket, hesitating, shot another glance under his glasses. "Do you allude to—a—revelations?"

"Very curious ones."

Mr. Locket, still on his feet, had kept his body at the bowing angle; it was therefore easy for him after an instant to bend a little further and to sink into his chair with a movement of his hand toward the seat Baron had occupied. Baron resumed possession of this convenience, and the conversation took a fresh start on a basis which such an extension of privilege could render but little less humiliating to our young man. He had matured no plan of confiding his secret to Mr. Locket, and he had really come out to make him conscientiously that other announcement as to which it appeared that so much artistic agitation had been wasted. He had indeed during the past days—days of painful indecision—appealed in imagination to the editor of the Promiscuous, as he had appealed to other sources of comfort; but his scruples turned their face upon him from quarters high as well as low, and if on the one hand he had by no means made up his mind not to mention his strange knowledge, he had still more left to the determination of the moment the question of how he should introduce the subject. He was in fact too nervous to decide; he only felt that he needed for his peace of mind to communicate his discovery. He wanted an opinion, the impression of somebody else, and even in this intensely professional presence, five minutes after he had begun to tell his queer story, he felt relieved of half his burden. His story was very queer; he could take the measure of that himself as he spoke; but wouldn't this very circumstance qualify it for the Promiscuous?

"Of course the letters may be forgeries," said Mr. Locket at last.

"I've no doubt that's what many people will say."

"Have they been seen by any expert?"

"No indeed; they've been seen by nobody."

"Have you got any of them with you?"

"No; I felt nervous about bringing them out."

"That's a pity. I should have liked the testimony of my eyes."

"You may have it if you'll come to my rooms. If you don't care to do that without a further guarantee I'll copy you out some passages."

"Select a few of the worst!" Mr. Locket laughed. Over Baron's distressing information he had become quite human and genial. But he added in a moment more dryly: "You know they ought to be seen by an expert."

"That's exactly what I dread," said Peter.

"They'll be worth nothing to me if they're not."

Peter communed with his innermost spirit. "How much will they be worth to *me* if they *are*?"

Mr. Locket turned in his study-chair. "I should require to look at them before answering that question."

"I've been to the British museum—there are many of his letters there. I've obtained permission to see them, and I've compared everything carefully. I repudiate the possibility of forgery. No sign of genuineness is wanting; there are details, down to the very postmarks, that no forger could have invented. Besides, whose interest could it conceivably have been? A labor of unspeakable difficulty, and all for what advantage? There are so many letters, too—twenty-seven in all."

"Lord, what an ass!" Mr. Locket exclaimed.

"It will be one of the strangest post-mortem revelations of which history preserves the record."

Mr. Locket, grave now, worried with a paper-knife the crevice of a drawer. "It's very odd. But to be worth anything such documents should be subjected to a searching criticism—I mean of the historical kind."

"Certainly; that would be the task of the writer introducing them to the public."

Again Mr. Locket considered; then with a smile he looked up. "You had better give up original composition and take to buying old furniture."

"Do you mean because it will pay better?"

"For you, I should think, original composition couldn't pay worse. The creative faculty's so rare."

"I do feel tempted to turn my attention to real heroes," Peter replied.

"I'm bound to declare that Sir Dominick Ferrand was never one of mine. Flashy, crafty, second-rate—that's how I've always read him. It was never a secret, moreover, that his private life had its weak spots. He was a mere flash in the pan."

"He speaks to the people of this country," said Baron.

"He did; but his voice—the voice, I mean, of his prestige—is scarcely audible now."

"They're still proud of some of the things he did at the Foreign Office—the famous 'exchange' with Spain, in the Mediterranean, which took Europe so by surprise and by which she felt injured, especially when it became apparent how much we had the best of the bargain. Then the sudden, unexpected show of force by which he imposed on the United States our interpretation of that tiresome treaty—I could never make out what it was about. These were both matters that no one really cared a straw about, but he made every one feel as if they cared; the nation rose to the way he played his trumps—it was uncommon. He was one of the few men we've had, in our period, who took Europe, or took America, by surprise, made them jump a bit; and the country liked his doing it—it was a pleasant change. The rest of the world considered that they knew in any case exactly what we would do, which was usually nothing at all. Say what you like, he's still a high name; partly also, no doubt, on account of other things his early success and early death, his political 'cheek' and wit; his very appearance—he certainly was handsome—and the possibilities (of future personal supremacy) which it was the fashion at the time, which it's the fashion still, to say had passed away with him. He had been twice at the Foreign Office; that alone was remarkable for a man dying at forty-four. What therefore will the country think when it learns he was venal?"

Peter Baron himself was not angry with Sir Dominick Ferrand, who had simply become to him (he had been "reading up" feverishly for a week) a very curious subject of psychological study; but he could easily put himself in the place of that portion of the public whose memory was long enough for their patriotism to receive a shock. It was some time fortunately since the conduct of public affairs had wanted for men of disinterested ability, but the extraordinary documents concealed (of all places in the world—it was as fantastic as a nightmare) in a "bargain" picked up at second-hand by an obscure scribbler, would be a calculable blow to the retrospective mind. Baron saw vividly that if these relics should be made public the scandal, the horror, the chatter would be immense. Immense would be also the contribution to truth, the rectification of history. He had felt for several days (and it was exactly what had made him so nervous) as if he held in his hand the key to public attention.

"There are too many things to explain," Mr. Locket went on, "and the singular *provenance* of your papers would count almost overwhelmingly against them even if the other objections were met. There would be a perfect and probably a very complicated pedigree to trace. How did they get into your davenport, as you call it, and how long had they been there? What hands secreted them? what hands had, so incredibly, clung to them and preserved them? Who are the persons mentioned in them? who are the correspondents, the parties to the nefarious transactions? You say the transactions appear to be of two distinct kinds—some of them connected with public business and others involving obscure personal relations."

"They all have this in common," said Peter Baron, "that they constitute evidence of uneasiness, in some instances of painful alarm, on the writer's part, in relation to exposure—the exposure in the one case, as I gather, of the fact that he had availed himself of official opportunities to promote enterprises (public works and that sort of thing) in which he had a pecuniary stake. The dread of the light in the other connection is evidently different, and these letters are the earliest in date. They are addressed to a woman, from whom he had evidently received money."

Mr. Locket wiped his glasses. "What woman?"

"I haven't the least idea. There are lots of questions I can't answer, of course; lots of identities I can't establish; lots of gaps I can't fill. But as to two points I'm clear, and they are the essential ones. In the first place the papers in my possession are genuine; in the second place they're compromising."

With this Peter Baron rose again, rather vexed with himself for having been led on to advertise his treasure (it was his interlocutor's perfectly natural scepticism that produced this effect), for he felt that he was putting himself in a false position. He detected in Mr. Locket's studied detachment the fermentation of impulses from which, unsuccessful as he was, he himself prayed to be delivered.

Mr. Locket remained seated; he watched Baron go across the room for his hat and umbrella. "Of course, the question would come up of whose property today such documents would legally he. There are heirs, descendants, executors to consider."

"In some degree perhaps; but I've gone into that a little. Sir Dominick Ferrand had no children, and he left no brothers and no sisters. His wife survived him, but she died ten years ago. He can have had no heirs and no executors to speak of, for he left no property."

"That's to his honour and against your theory," said Mr. Locket.

"I *have* no theory. He left a largeish mass of debt," Peter Baron added. At this Mr. Locket got up, while his visitor pursued: "So far as I can ascertain, though of course my inquiries have had to be very rapid and superficial, there is no one now living, directly or indirectly related to the personage in question, who would be likely to suffer from any steps in the direction of publicity. It happens to be a rare instance of a life that had, as it were, no loose ends. At least there are none perceptible at present."

"I see, I see," said Mr. Locket. "But I don't think I should care much for your article."

"What article?"

"The one you seem to wish to write, embodying this new matter."

"Oh, I don't wish to write it!" Peter exclaimed. And then he bade his host good-by.

"Good-by," said Mr. Locket. "Mind you, I don't say that I think there's nothing in it."

"You would think there was something in it if you were to see my documents."

"I should like to see the secret compartment," the caustic editor rejoined. "Copy me out some extracts."

"To what end, if there's no question of their being of use to you?"

"I don't say that—I might like the letters themselves."

"Themselves?"

"Not as the basis of a paper, but just to publish—for a sensation."

"They'd sell your number!" Baron laughed.

"I daresay I should like to look at them," Mr. Locket conceded after a moment. "When should I find you at home?"

"Don't come," said the young man. "I make you no offer."

"I might make *you* one," the editor hinted. "Don't trouble yourself; I shall probably destroy them." With this Peter Baron took his departure, waiting however just afterwards, in the street near the house, as if he had been looking out for a stray hansom, to which he would not have signalled had it appeared. He thought Mr. Locket might hurry after him, but Mr. Locket seemed to have other things to do, and Peter Baron returned on foot to Jersey Villas.

IV.

ON the evening that succeeded this apparently pointless encounter he had an interview more conclusive with Mrs. Bundy, for whose shrewd and philosophic view of life he had several times expressed, even to the good woman herself, a considerable relish. The situation at Jersey Villas (Mrs. Ryves had suddenly flown off to Dover) was such as to create in him a desire for moral support, and there was a kind of domestic determination in Mrs. Bundy which seemed, in general, to advertise it. He had asked for her on coming in, but had been told she was absent for the hour; upon which he had addressed himself mechanically to the task of doing up his dishonoured manuscript—the ingenious fiction about which Mr. Locket had been so stupid—for further adventures and not improbable defeats. He passed a restless, ineffective afternoon, asking himself if his genius were a horrid delusion, looking out of his window for something that didn't happen, something that seemed now to be the advent of a persuasive Mr. Locket and now the return, from an absence more disappointing even than Mrs. Bundy's, of his interesting neighbour of the parlours. He was so nervous and so depressed that he was unable even to fix his mind on the composition of the note with which, on its next peregrination, it was necessary that his manuscript should be accompanied. He was too nervous to eat, and he forgot even to dine; he forgot to light his candles, he let his fire go out, and it was in the melancholy chill of the late dusk that Mrs. Bundy, arriving at last with his lamp, found him extended moodily upon his sofa. She had been informed that he wished to speak to her, and as she placed on the malodorous luminary an oily shade of green pasteboard she expressed the friendly hope that there was nothing wrong with his 'ealth.

The young man rose from his couch, pulling himself together sufficiently to reply that his health was well enough but that his spirits were down in his hoots. He had a strong disposition to "draw" his landlady on the subject of Mrs. Ryves, as well as a vivid conviction that she constituted a theme as to which Mrs. Bundy would require little pressure to tell him even more than she knew. At the same time he hated to appear to pry into the secrets of his absent friend; to discuss her with their bustling hostess resembled too much for his taste a gossip with a tattling servant about an unconscious employer. He left out of account however Mrs. Bundy's knowledge of the human heart, for it was this fine principle that broke down the barriers after he had reflected reassuringly that it was not meddling with Mrs. Ryves's affairs to try and find out if she struck such an observer as happy. Crudely, abruptly, even a little blushingly, he put the direct question to Mrs. Bundy, and this led tolerably straight to another question, which, on his spirit, sat equally heavy (they were indeed but different phases of the same), and which the good woman answered with expression when she ejaculated: "Think it a liberty for you to run down for a few hours? If she do, my dear sir, just send her to me to talk to!" As regards happiness indeed she warned Baron against imposing too high a standard on a young thing who had been through so much, and before he knew it he found himself, without the responsibility of choice, in submissive receipt of Mrs. Bundy's version of this experience. It was an interesting picture, though it had its infirmities, one of them congenital and consisting of the fact that it had sprung essentially from the virginal brain of Miss Teagle. Amplified, edited, embellished by the richer genius of Mrs. Bundy, who had incorporated with it and now liberally introduced copious interleavings of Miss Teagle's own romance, it gave Peter Baron much food for meditation, at the same time that it only half relieved his curiosity about the causes of the charming woman's underlying strangeness. He sounded this note experimentally in Mrs. Bundy's ear, but it was easy to see that it didn't reverberate in her fancy. She had no idea of the picture it would have been natural for him to desire that Mrs. Ryves should present to him, and she was therefore unable to estimate the points in respect to which his actual impression was irritating. She had indeed no adequate conception of the intellectual requirements of a young man in love. She couldn't tell him why their faultless friend was so isolated, so unrelated, so nervously, shrinkingly proud. On the other hand she could tell him (he knew it already) that she had passed many years of her life in the acquisition of accomplishments at a seat of learning no less remote than Boulogne, and that Miss Teagle had been intimately acquainted with the late Mr. Everard Ryves, who was a "most rising" young man in the city, not making any year less than his clear twelve hundred. "Now that he isn't there to make them, his mourning widow can't live as she had then, can she?" Mrs. Bundy asked.

Baron was not prepared to say that she could, but he thought of another way she might live as he sat, the next day, in the train which rattled him down to Dover. The place, as he approached it, seemed bright and breezy to him; his roamings had been neither far enough nor frequent enough to make the cockneyfied coast insipid. Mrs. Bundy had of course given him the address he needed, and on emerging from the station he was on the point of asking what direction he should take. His attention however at this moment was drawn away by the bustle of the departing boat. He had been long enough shut up in London to be conscious of refreshment in the mere act of turning his face to Paris. He wandered off to the pier in company with happier tourists and, leaning on a rail, watched enviously the preparation, the agitation of foreign travel. It was for some minutes a foretaste of adventure; but, ah, when was he to have the very draught? He turned away as he dropped this interrogative sigh, and in doing so perceived that in another part of the pier two ladies and a little boy were gathered with something of the same wistfulness. The little boy indeed happened to look round for a moment, upon which, with the keenness of the predatory age, he recognised in our young man a source of pleasures from which he lately had been weaned. He bounded forward with irrepressible cries of "Geegee!" and Peter lifted him aloft for an embrace. On putting him down the pilgrim from Jersey Villas stood confronted with a sensibly severe Miss Teagle, who had followed her little charge. "What's the matter with the old woman?" he asked himself as he offered her a hand which she treated as the merest detail. Whatever it was, it was (and very properly, on the part of a loyal *suivante*) the same complaint as that of her employer, to whom, from a distance, for Mrs. Ryves had not advanced an inch, he flourished his hat as she stood looking at him with a face that he imagined rather white. Mrs. Ryves's response to this salutation was to shift her position in such a manner as to appear again absorbed in the Calais boat. Peter Baron, however, kept hold of the child, whom Miss Teagle artfully endeavoured to wrest from him—a policy in which he was aided by Sidney's own rough but instinctive loyalty; and he was thankful for the happy effect of being dragged by his jubilant friend in the very direction in which he had tended for so many hours. Mrs. Ryves turned once more as he came near, and then, from the sweet, strained smile with which she asked him if he were on his way to France, he saw that if she had been angry at his having followed her she had quickly got over it.

"No, I'm not crossing; but it came over me that you might be, and that's why I hurried down—to catch you before you were off."

"Oh, we can't go—more's the pity; but why, if we could," Mrs. Ryves inquired, "should you wish to prevent it?"

"Because I've something to ask you first, something that may take some time." He saw now that her embarrassment had really not been resentful; it had been nervous, tremulous, as the emotion of an unexpected pleasure might have been. "That's really why I determined last night, without asking your leave first to pay you this little visit—that and the intense desire for another bout of horse-play with Sidney. Oh, I've come to see you," Peter Baron went on, "and I won't make any secret of the fact that I expect you to resign yourself gracefully to the trial and give me all your time. The day's lovely, and I'm ready to declare that the place is as good as the day. Let me drink deep of these things, drain the cup like a man who hasn't been out of London for months and months. Let me walk with you and talk with you and lunch with you—I go back this afternoon. Give me all your hours in short, so that they may live in my memory as one of the sweetest occasions of life."

The emission of steam from the French packet made such an uproar that Baron could breathe his passion into the young woman's ear without scandalising the spectators; and the charm which little by little it scattered over his fleeting visit proved indeed to be the collective influence of the conditions he had put into words. "What is it you wish to ask me?" Mrs. Ryves demanded, as they stood there together; to which he replied that he would tell her all about it if she would send Miss Teagle off with Sidney. Miss Teagle, who was always anticipating her cue, had already begun ostentatiously to gaze at the distant shores of France and was easily enough induced to take an earlier start home and rise to the responsibility of stopping on her way to contend with the butcher. She had however to retire without Sidney, who clung to his recovered prey, so that the rest of the episode was seasoned, to Baron's sense, by the importunate twitch of the child's little, plump, cool hand. The friends wandered together with a conjugal air and Sidney not between them, hanging wistfully, first, over the lengthened picture of the Calais boat, till they could look after it, as it moved rumbling away, in a spell of silence which seemed to confess—especially when, a moment later, their eyes met—that it produced the same fond fancy in each. The presence of the boy moreover was no hindrance to their talking in a manner that they made believe was very frank. Peter Baron presently told his companion what it was he had taken a journey to ask, and he had time afterwards to get over his discomfiture at her appearance of having fancied it might be something greater. She seemed disappointed (but she was forgiving) on learning from him that he had only wished to know if she judged ferociously his not having complied with her request to respect certain seals.

"How ferociously do you suspect me of having judged it?" she inquired.

"Why, to the extent of leaving the house the next moment."

They were still lingering on the great granite pier when he touched on this matter, and she sat down at the end while the breeze, warmed by the sunshine, ruffled the purple sea. She coloured a little and looked troubled, and after an instant she repeated interrogatively: "The next moment?"

"As soon as I told you what I had done. I was scrupulous about this, you will remember; I went straight downstairs to confess to you. You turned away from me, saying nothing; I couldn't imagine—as I vow I can't imagine now—why such a matter should appear so closely to touch you. I went out on some business and when I returned you had quitted the house. It had all the look of my having offended you, of your wishing to get away from me. You didn't even give me time to tell you how it was that, in spite of your advice, I determined to see for myself what my discovery represented. You must do me justice and hear what determined me."

Mrs. Ryves got up from her scat and asked him, as a particular favour, not to allude again to his discovery. It was no concern of hers at all, and she had no warrant for prying into his secrets. She was very sorry to have been for a moment so absurd as to appear to do so, and she humbly begged his pardon for her meddling. Saying this she walked on with a charming colour in her cheek, while he laughed out, though he was really bewildered, at the endless capriciousness of women. Fortunately the incident didn't spoil the hour, in which there were other sources of satisfaction, and they took their course to her lodgings with such pleasant little pauses and excursions by the way as permitted her to show him the objects of interest at Dover. She let him stop at a wine-merchant's and buy a bottle for luncheon, of which, in its order, they partook, together with a pudding invented by Miss Teagle, which, as they hypocritically swallowed it, made them look at each other in an intimacy of indulgence. They came out again and, while Sidney grubbed in the gravel of the shore, sat selfishly on the Parade, to the disappointment of Miss Teagle, who had fixed her hopes on a fly and a ladylike visit to the castle. Baron had his eye on his watch—he had to think of his train and the dismal return and many other melancholy things; but the sea in the afternoon light was a more appealing picture; the wind had gone down, the Channel was crowded, the sails of the ships were white in the purple distance. The young man had asked his companion (he had asked her before) when she was to come back to Jersey Villas, and she had said that she should probably stay at Dover another week. It was dreadfully expensive, but it was doing the child all the good in the world, and if Miss Teagle could go up for some things she should probably be able to manage an extension. Earlier in the day she had said that she perhaps wouldn't return to Jersey Villas at all, or only return to wind up her connection with Mrs. Bundy. At another moment she had spoken of an early date, an immediate reoccupation of the wonderful parlours. Baron saw that she had no plan, no real reasons, that she was vague and, in secret, worried and nervous, waiting for something that didn't depend on herself. A silence of several minutes had fallen upon them while they watched the shining sails; to which Mrs. Ryves put an end by exclaiming abruptly, but without completing her sentence: "Oh, if you had come to tell me you had destroyed them—"

"Those terrible papers? I like the way you talk about 'destroying!' You don't even know what they are."

"I don't want to know; they put me into a state."

"What sort of a state?"

"I don't know; they haunt me."

"They haunted me; that was why, early one morning, suddenly, I couldn't keep my hands off them. I had told you I wouldn't touch them. I had deferred to your whim, your superstition (what is it?) but at last they got the better of me. I had lain awake all night threshing about, itching with curiosity. It made me ill; my own nerves (as I may say) were irritated, my capacity to work was gone. It had come over me in the small hours in the shape of an obsession, a fixed idea, that there was nothing in the ridiculous relics and that my exaggerated scruples were making a fool of me. It was ten to one they were rubbish, they were vain, they were empty; that they had been even a practical joke on the part of some weak-minded gentleman of leisure, the former possessor of the confounded davenport. The longer I hovered about them with such precautions the longer I was taken in, and the sooner I exposed their insignificance the sooner I should get back to my usual occupations. This conviction made my hand so uncontrollable that that morning before breakfast I broke one of the seals. It took me but a few minutes to perceive that the contents were not rubbish; the little bundle contained old letters—very curious old letters."

"I know—I know; 'private and confidential.' So you broke the other seals?" Mrs. Ryves looked at him with the strange apprehension he had seen in her eyes when she appeared at his door the moment after his discovery.

"You know, of course, because I told you an hour later, though you would let me tell you very little."

Baron, as he met this queer gaze, smiled hard at her to prevent her guessing that he smarted with the fine reproach conveyed in the tone of her last words; but she appeared able to guess everything, for she reminded him that she had not had to wait that morning till he came downstairs to know what had happened above, but had shown him at the moment how she had been conscious of it an hour before, had passed on her side the same tormented night as he, and had had to exert extraordinary self-command not to rush up to his rooms while the study of the open packets was going on. "You're so sensitively organised and you've such mysterious powers that you re uncanny," Baron declared.

"I feel what takes place at a distance; that's all."

"One would think somebody you liked was in danger."

"I told you that that was what was present to me the day I came up to see you."

"Oh, but you don't like me so much as that," Baron argued, laughing.

She hesitated. "No, I don't know that I do."

"It must be for someone else—the other person concerned. The other day, however, you wouldn't let me tell you that person's name."

Mrs. Ryves, at this, rose quickly. "I don't want to know it; it's none of my business."

"No, fortunately, I don't think it is," Baron rejoined, walking with her along the Parade. She had Sidney by the hand now, and the young man was on the other side of her. They moved toward the station—she had offered to go part of the way. "But with your miraculous gift it's a wonder you haven't divined."

"I only divine what I want," said Mrs. Ryves.

"That's very convenient!" exclaimed Peter, to whom Sidney had presently come round again. "Only, being thus in the dark, it's difficult to see your motive for wishing the papers destroyed."

Mrs. Ryves meditated, looking fixedly at the ground. "I thought you might do it to oblige me."

"Does it strike you that such an expectation, formed in such conditions, is reasonable?"

Mrs. Ryves stopped short, and this time she turned on him the clouded clearness of her eyes. "What do you mean to do with them?"

It was Peter Baron's turn to meditate, which he did, on the empty asphalt of the Parade (the "season," at Dover, was not yet), where their shadows were long in the afternoon light. He was under such a charm as he had never known, and he wanted immensely to be able to reply: "I'll do anything you like if you'll love me." These words, however, would have represented a responsibility and have constituted what was vulgarly termed an offer. An offer of what? he quickly asked himself here, as he had already asked himself after making in spirit other awkward dashes in the same direction—of what but his poverty, his obscurity, his attempts that had come to nothing, his abilities for which there was nothing to show? Mrs. Ryves was not exactly a success, but she was a greater success than Peter Baron. Poor as he was he hated the sordid (he knew she didn't love it), and he felt small for talking of marriage. Therefore he didn't put the question in the words it would have pleased him most to hear himself utter, but he compromised, with an angry young pang, and said to her: "What will you do for me if I put an end to them?"

She shook her head sadly—it was always her prettiest movement. "I can promise nothing—oh, no, I can't promise! We must part now," she added. "You'll miss your train."

He looked at his watch, taking the hand she held out to him. She drew it away quickly, and nothing then was left him, before hurrying to the station, but to catch up Sidney and squeeze him till he uttered a little shriek. On the way back to town the situation struck him as grotesque.

V.

IT tormented him so the next morning that after threshing it out a little further he felt he had something of a grievance. Mrs. Ryves's intervention had made him acutely uncomfortable, for she had taken the attitude of exerting pressure without, it appeared, recognising on his part an equal right. She had imposed herself as an influence, yet she held herself aloof as a participant; there were things she looked to him to do for her, yet she could tell him of no good that would come to him from the doing. She should either have had less to say or have been willing to say more, and he asked himself why he should be the sport of her moods and her mysteries. He perceived her knack of punctual interference to be striking, but it was just this apparent infallibility that he resented. Why didn't she set up at once as a professional clairvoyant and eke out her little income more successfully? In purely private life such a gift was disconcerting; her divinations, her evasions disturbed at any rate his own tranquillity.

What disturbed it still further was that he received early in the day a visit from Mr. Locket, who, leaving him under no illusion as to the grounds of such an honour, remarked as soon as he had got into the room or rather while he still panted on the second flight and the smudged little slavey held open Baron's door, that he had taken up his young friend's invitation to look at Sir Dominick Ferrand's letters for himself. Peter drew them forth with a promptitude intended to show that he recognised the commercial character of the call and without attenuating the inconsequence of this departure from the last determination he had expressed to Mr. Locket. He showed his visitor the davenport and the hidden recess, and he smoked a cigarette, humming softly, with a sense of unwonted advantage and triumph, while the cautious editor sat silent and handled the papers. For all his caution Mr. Locket was unable to keep a warmer light out of his judicial eye as he said to Baron at last with sociable brevity—a tone that took many things for granted: "I'll take them home with me—they require much attention."

The young man looked at him a moment. "Do you think they're genuine?" He didn't mean to be mocking, he meant not to be; but the words sounded so to his own ear, and he could see that they produced that effect on Mr. Locket.

"I can't in the least determine. I shall have to go into them at my leisure, and that's why I ask you to lend them to me."

He had shuffled the papers together with a movement charged, while he spoke, with the air of being preliminary to that of thrusting them into a little black bag which he had brought with him and which, resting on the shelf of the davenport, struck Peter, who viewed it askance, as an object darkly editorial. It made our young man, somehow, suddenly apprehensive; the advantage of which he had just been conscious was about to be transferred by a quiet process of legerdemain to a person who already had advantages enough. Baron, in short, felt a deep pang of anxiety; he couldn't have said why. Mr. Locket took decidedly too many things for granted, and the explorer of Sir Dominick Ferrand's irregularities remembered afresh how clear he had been after all about his indisposition to traffic in them. He asked his visitor to what end he wished to remove the letters, since on the one hand there was no question now of the article in the Promiscuous which was to reveal their existence, and on the other he himself, as their owner, had a thousand insurmountable scruples about putting them into circulation.

Mr. Locket looked over his spectacles as over the battlements of a fortress. "I'm not thinking of the end—I'm thinking of the beginning. A few glances have assured me that such documents ought to be submitted to some competent eye."

"Oh, you mustn't show them to anyone!" Baron exclaimed.

"You may think me presumptuous, but the eye that I venture to allude to in those terms—"

"Is the eye now fixed so terribly on *me*?" Peter laughingly interrupted. "Oh, it would be interesting, I confess, to know how they strike a man of your acuteness!" It had occurred to him that by such a concession he might endear himself to a literary umpire hitherto implacable. There would be no question of his publishing Sir Dominick Ferrand, but he might, in due acknowledgment of services rendered, form the habit of publishing Peter Baron. "How long would it be your idea to retain them?" he inquired, in a manner which, he immediately became aware, was what incited Mr. Locket to begin stuffing the papers into his bag. With this perception he came quickly closer and, laying his hand on the gaping receptacle, lightly drew its two lips together. In this way the two men stood for a few seconds, touching, almost in the attitude of combat, looking hard into each other's eyes.

The tension was quickly relieved however by the surprised flush which mantled on Mr. Locket's brow. He fell back a few steps with an injured dignity that might have been a protest against physical violence. "Really, my dear young sir, your attitude is tantamount to an accusation of intended bad faith. Do you think I want to steal the confounded things?" In reply to such a challenge Peter could only hastily declare that he was guilty of no discourteous suspicion—he only wanted a limit named, a pledge of every precaution against accident. Mr. Locket admitted the justice of the demand, assured him he would restore the property within three days, and completed, with Peter's assistance, his little arrangements for removing it discreetly. When he was ready, his treacherous reticule distended with its treasures, he gave a lingering look at the inscrutable davenport. "It's how they ever got into that thing that puzzles one's brain!"

"There was some concatenation of circumstances that would doubtless seem natural enough if it were explained, but that one would have to remount the stream of time to ascertain. To one course I have definitely made up my mind: not to make any statement or any inquiry at the shop. I simply accept the mystery," said Peter, rather grandly.

"That would be thought a cheap escape if you were to put it into a story," Mr. Locket smiled.

"Yes, I shouldn't offer the story to *you*. I shall be impatient till I see my papers again," the young man called out, as his visitor hurried downstairs.

That evening, by the last delivery, he received, under the Dover postmark, a letter that was not from Miss Teagle. It was a slightly confused but altogether friendly note, written that morning after breakfast, the ostensible purpose of which was to thank him for the amiability of his visit, to express regret at any appearance the writer might have had of meddling with what didn't concern her, and to let him know that the evening before, after he had left her, she had in a moment of inspiration got hold of the tail of a really musical idea—a perfect accompaniment for the song he had so kindly given her. She had scrawled, as a specimen, a few bars at the end of her note, mystic, mocking musical signs which had no sense for her correspondent. The whole letter testified to a restless but rather pointless desire to remain in communication with him. In answering her, however, which he did that night before going to bed, it was on this bright possibility of their collaboration, its advantages for the future of each of them, that Baron principally expatiated. He spoke of this future with an eloquence of which he would have defended the sincerity, and drew of it a picture extravagantly rich. The next morning, as he was about to settle himself to tasks for some time terribly neglected, with a sense that after all it was rather a relief not to be sitting so close to Sir Dominick Ferrand, who had become dreadfully distracting; at the very moment at which he habitually addressed his preliminary invocation to the muse, he was agitated by the arrival of a telegram which proved to be an urgent request from Mr. Locket that he would immediately come down and see him. This represented, for poor Baron, whose funds were very low, another morning sacrificed, but somehow it didn't even occur to him that he might impose his own time upon the editor of the Promiscuous, the keeper of the keys of renown. He had some of the plasticity of the raw contributor. He gave the muse another holiday, feeling she was really ashamed to take it, and in course of time found himself in Mr. Locket's own chair at Mr. Locket's own table—so much nobler an expanse than the slippery slope of the davenport—considering with quick intensity, in the white flash of certain words just brought out by his host, the quantity of happiness, of emancipation that might reside in a hundred pounds.

Yes, that was what it meant: Mr. Locket, in the twenty-four hours, had discovered so much in Sir Dominick's literary remains that his visitor found him primed with an offer. A hundred pounds would be paid him that day, that minute, and no questions would be either asked or answered. "I take all the risks, I take all the risks," the editor of the Promiscuous repeated. The letters were out on the table, Mr. Locket was on the hearthrug, like an orator on a platform, and Peter, under the influence of his sudden ultimatum, had dropped, rather weakly, into the seat which happened to be nearest and which, as he became conscious it moved on a pivot, he whirled round so as to enable himself to look at his tempter with an eye intended to be cold. What surprised him most was to find Mr. Locket taking exactly the line about the expediency of publication which he would have expected Mr. Locket not to take. "Hush it all up; a barren scandal, an offence that can't be remedied, is the thing in the world that least justifies an airing—" some such line as that was the line he would have thought natural to a man whose life was spent in weighing questions of propriety and who had only the other day objected, in the light of this virtue, to a work of the most disinterested art. But the author of that incorruptible masterpiece had put his finger on the place in saying to his interlocutor on the occasion of his last visit that, if given to the world in the pages of the Promiscuous, Sir Dominick's aberrations would sell the edition. It was not necessary for Mr. Locket to reiterate to his young friend his phrase about their making a sensation. If he wished to purchase the "rights," as theatrical people said, it was not to protect a celebrated name or to lock them up in a cupboard. That formula of Baron's covered all the ground, and one edition was a low estimate of the probable performance of the magazine.

Peter left the letters behind him and, on withdrawing from the editorial presence, took a long walk on the Embankment. His impressions were at war with each other—he was flurried by possibilities of which he yet denied the existence. He had consented to trust Mr. Locket with the papers a day or two longer, till he should have thought out the terms on which he might—in the event of certain occurrences—be induced to dispose of them. A hundred pounds were not this gentleman's last word, nor perhaps was mere unreasoning intractability Peter's own. He sighed as he took no note of the pictures made by barges—sighed because it all might mean money. He needed money bitterly; he owed it in disquieting quarters. Mr. Locket had put it before him that he had a high responsibility—that he might vindicate the disfigured truth, contribute a chapter to the history of England. "You haven't a right to suppress such momentous facts," the hungry little editor had declared, thinking how the series (he would spread it into three numbers) would be the talk of the town. If Peter had money he might treat himself to ardour, to bliss. Mr. Locket had said, no doubt justly enough, that there were ever so many questions one would have to meet should one venture to play so daring a game. These questions, embarrassments, dangers—the danger, for instance, of the cropping-up of some lurking litigious relative—he would take over unreservedly and bear the brunt of dealing with. It was to be remembered that the papers were discredited, vitiated by their childish pedigree; such a preposterous origin, suggesting, as he had hinted before, the feeble ingenuity of a third-rate novelist, was a thing he should have to place himself at the positive disadvantage of being silent about. He would rather give no account of the matter at all than expose himself to the ridicule that such a story would infallibly excite. Couldn't one see them in advance, the clever, taunting things the daily and weekly papers would say? Peter Baron had his guileless side, but he felt, as he worried with a stick that betrayed him the granite parapets of the Thames, that he was not such a fool as not to know how Mr. Locket would "work" the mystery of his marvellous find. Nothing could help it on better with the public than the impenetrability of the secret attached to it. If Mr. Locket should only be able to kick up dust enough over the circumstances that had guided his hand his fortune would literally be made. Peter thought a hundred pounds a low bid, yet he wondered how the Promiscuous could bring itself to offer such a sum—so large it loomed in the light of literary remuneration as hitherto revealed to our young man. The explanation of this anomaly was of course that the editor shrewdly saw a dozen ways of getting his money back. There would be in the "sensation," at a later stage, the making of a book in large type—the book of the hour; and the profits of this scandalous volume or, if one preferred the name, this reconstruction, before an impartial posterity, of a great historical humbug, the sum "down," in other words, that any lively publisher would give for it, figured vividly in Mr. Locket's calculations. It was therefore altogether an opportunity of dealing at first hand with the lively publisher that Peter was invited to forego. Peter gave a masterful laugh, rejoicing in his heart that, on the spot, in the *repaire* he had lately quitted, he had not been tempted by a figure that would have approximately represented the value of his property. It was a good job, he mentally added as he turned his face homeward, that there was so little likelihood of his having to struggle with that particular pressure.

VI.

When, half an hour later, he approached Jersey Villas, he noticed that the house-door was open; then, as he reached the gate, saw it make a frame for an unexpected presence. Mrs. Ryves, in her bonnet and jacket, looked out from it as if she were expecting something—as if she had been passing to and fro to watch. Yet when he had expressed to her that it was a delightful welcome she replied that she had only thought there might possibly be a cab in sight. He offered to go and look for one, upon which it appeared that after all she was not, as yet at least, in need. He went back with her into her sitting-room, where she let him know that within a couple of days she had seen clearer what was best; she had determined to quit Jersey Villas and had come up to take away her things, which she had just been packing and getting together.

"I wrote you last night a charming letter in answer to yours," Baron said. "You didn't mention in yours that you were coming up."

"It wasn't your answer that brought me. It hadn't arrived when I came away."

"You'll see when you get back that my letter is charming."

"I daresay." Baron had observed that the room was not, as she had intimated, in confusion—Mrs. Ryves's preparations for departure were not striking. She saw him look round and, standing in front of the fireless grate with her hands behind her, she suddenly asked: "Where have you come from now?"

"From an interview with a literary friend."

"What are you concocting between you?"

"Nothing at all. We've fallen out—we don't agree."

"Is he a publisher?"

"He's an editor."

"Well, I'm glad you don't agree. I don't know what he wants, but, whatever it is, don't do it."

"He must do what *I* want!" said Baron.

"And what's that?"

"Oh, I'll tell you when he has done it!" Baron begged her to let him hear the "musical idea" she had mentioned in her letter; on which she took off her hat and jacket and, seating herself at her piano, gave him, with a sentiment of which the very first notes thrilled him, the accompaniment of his song. She phrased the words with her sketchy sweetness, and he sat there as if he had been held in a velvet vise, throbbing with the emotion, irrecoverable ever after in its freshness, of the young artist in the presence for the first time of "production"—the proofs of his book, the hanging of his picture, the rehearsal of his play. When she had finished he asked again for the same delight, and then for more music and for more; it did him such a world of good, kept him quiet and safe, smoothed out the creases of his spirit. She dropped her own experiments and gave him immortal things, and he lounged there, pacified and charmed, feeling the mean little room grow large and vague and happy possibilities come back. Abruptly, at the piano, she called out to him: "Those papers of yours—the letters you found—are not in the house?"

"No, they're not in the house."

"I was sure of it! No matter—it's all right!" she added. She herself was pacified—trouble was a false note. Later he was on the point of asking her how she knew the objects she had mentioned were not in the house; but he let it pass. The subject was a profitless riddle—a puzzle that grew grotesquely bigger, like some monstrosity seen in the darkness, as one opened one's eyes to it. He closed his eyes—he wanted another vision. Besides, she had shown him that she had extraordinary senses—her explanation would have been stranger than the fact. Moreover they had other things to talk about, in particular the question of her putting off her return to Dover till the morrow and dispensing meanwhile with the valuable protection of Sidney. This was indeed but another face of the question of her dining with him somewhere that evening (where else should she dine?)—accompanying him, for instance, just for an hour of Bohemia, in their deadly respectable lives, to a jolly little place in Soho. Mrs. Ryves declined to have her life abused, but in fact, at the proper moment, at the jolly little place, to which she did accompany him—it dealt in macaroni and Chianti—the pair put their elbows on the crumpled cloth and, face to face, with their little emptied coffee-cups pushed away and the young man's cigarette lighted by her command, became increasingly confidential. They went afterwards to the theatre, in cheap places, and came home in "busses" and under umbrellas.

On the way back Peter Baron turned something over in his mind as he had never turned anything before; it was the question of whether, at the end, she would let him come into her sitting-room for five minutes. He felt on this point a passion of suspense and impatience, and yet for what would it be but to tell her how poor he was? This was literally the moment to say it, so supremely depleted had the hour of Bohemia left him. Even Bohemia was too expensive, and yet in the course of the day his whole temper on the subject of certain fitnesses had changed. At Jersey Villas (it was near midnight, and Mrs. Ryves, scratching a light for her glimmering taper, had said: "Oh, yes, come in for a minute if you like!"), in her precarious parlour, which was indeed, after the brilliances of the evening, a return to ugliness and truth, she let him stand while he explained that he had certainly everything in the way of fame and fortune still to gain, but that youth and love and faith and energy—to say nothing of her supreme dearness—were all on his side. Why, if one's beginnings were rough, should one add to the hardness of the conditions by giving up the dream which, if she would only hear him out, would make just the blessed difference? Whether Mrs. Ryves heard him out or not is a circumstance as to which this chronicle happens to be silent; but after he had got possession of both her hands and breathed into her face for a moment all the intensity of his tenderness—in the relief and joy of utterance he felt it carry him like a rising flood—she checked him with better reasons, with a cold, sweet afterthought in which he felt there was something deep. Her procrastinating head-shake was prettier than ever, yet it had never meant so many fears and pains—impossibilities and memories, independences and pieties, and a sort of uncomplaining ache for the ruin of a friendship that had been happy. She had liked him—if she hadn't she wouldn't have let him think so!—but she protested that she had not, in the odious vulgar sense, "encouraged" him. Moreover she couldn't talk of such things in that place, at that hour, and she begged him not to make her regret her good-nature in staying over. There were peculiarities in her position, considerations insurmountable. She got rid of him with kind and confused words, and afterwards, in the dull, humiliated night, he felt that he had been put in his place. Women in her situation, women who after having really loved and lost, usually lived on into the new dawns in which old ghosts steal away. But there was something in his whimsical neighbour that struck him as terribly invulnerable.

VII.

"I've had time to look a little further into what we're prepared to do, and I find the case is one in which I should consider the advisability of going to an extreme length," said Mr. Locket. Jersey Villas the next morning had had the privilege of again receiving the editor of the Promiscuous, and he sat once more at the davenport, where the bone of contention, in the shape of a large, loose heap of papers that showed how much they had been handled, was placed well in view. "We shall see our way to offering you three hundred, but we shouldn't, I must positively assure you, see it a single step further."

Peter Baron, in his dressing-gown and slippers, with his hands in his pockets, crept softly about the room, repeating, below his breath and with inflections that for his own sake he endeavoured to make humorous: "Three hundred—three hundred." His state of mind was far from hilarious, for he felt poor and sore and disappointed; but he wanted to prove to himself that he was gallant—was made, in general and in particular, of undiscourageable stuff. The first thing he had been aware of on stepping into his front room was that a four-wheeled cab, with Mrs. Ryves's luggage upon it, stood at the door of No. 3. Permitting himself, behind his curtain, a pardonable peep, he saw the mistress of his thoughts come out of the house, attended by Mrs. Bundy, and take her place in the modest vehicle. After this his eyes rested for a long time on the sprigged cotton back of the landlady, who kept bobbing at the window of the cab an endlessly moralising old head. Mrs. Ryves had really taken flight—he had made Jersey Villas impossible for her—but Mrs. Bundy, with a magnanimity unprecedented in the profession, seemed to express a belief in the purity of her motives. Baron felt that his own separation had been, for the present at least, effected; every instinct of delicacy prompted him to stand back.

Mr. Locket talked a long time, and Peter Baron listened and waited. He reflected that his willingness to listen would probably excite hopes in his visitor—hopes which he himself was ready to contemplate without a scruple.

He felt no pity for Mr. Locket and had no consideration for his suspense or for his possible illusions; he only felt sick and forsaken and in want of comfort and of money. Yet it was a kind of outrage to his dignity to have the knife held to his throat, and he was irritated above all by the ground on which Mr. Locket put the question—the ground of a service rendered to historical truth. It might be—he wasn't clear; it might be—the question was deep, too deep, probably, for his wisdom; at any rate he had to control himself not to interrupt angrily such dry, interested palaver, the false voice of commerce and of cant. He stared tragically out of the window and saw the stupid rain begin to fall; the day was duller even than his own soul, and Jersey Villas looked so sordidly hideous that it was no wonder Mrs. Ryves couldn't endure them. Hideous as they were he should have to tell Mrs. Bundy in the course of the day that he was obliged to seek humbler quarters. Suddenly he interrupted Mr. Locket; he observed to him: "I take it that if I should make you this concession the hospitality of the Promiscuous would be by that very fact unrestrictedly secured to me."

Mr. Locket stared. "Hospitality—secured?" He thumbed the proposition as if it were a hard peach.

"I mean that of course you wouldn't—in courtsey, in gratitude—keep on declining my things."

"I should give them my best attention—as I've always done in the past."

Peter Baron hesitated. It was a case in which there would have seemed to be some chance for the ideally shrewd aspirant in such an advantage as he possessed; but after a moment the blood rushed into his face with the shame of the idea of pleading for his productions in the name of anything but their merit. It was as if he had stupidly uttered evil of them. Nevertheless be added the interrogation:

"Would you for instance publish my little story?"

"The one I read (and objected to some features of) the other day? Do you mean—a—with the alteration?" Mr. Locket continued.

"Oh, no, I mean utterly without it. The pages you want altered contain, as I explained to you very lucidly, I think, the very *raison d'être* of the work, and it would therefore, it seems to me, be an imbecility of the first magnitude to cancel them." Peter had really renounced all hope that his critic would understand what he meant, but, under favour of circumstances, he couldn't forbear to taste the luxury, which probably never again would come within his reach, of being really plain, for one wild moment, with an editor.

Mr. Locket gave a constrained smile. "Think of the scandal, Mr. Baron."

"But isn't this other scandal just what you're going in for?"

"It will be a great public service."

"You mean it will be a big scandal, whereas my poor story would be a very small one, and that it's only out of a big one that money's to be made."

Mr. Locket got up—he too had his dignity to vindicate. "Such a sum as I offer you ought really to be an offset against all claims."

"Very good—I don't mean to make any, since you don't really care for what I write. I take note of your offer," Peter pursued, "and I engage to give you to-night (in a few words left by my own hand at your house) my absolutely definite and final reply."

Mr. Locket's movements, as he hovered near the relics of the eminent statesman, were those of some feathered parent fluttering over a threatened nest. If he had brought his huddled brood back with him this morning it was because he had felt sure enough of closing the bargain to be able to be graceful. He kept a glittering eye on the papers and remarked that he was afraid that before leaving them he must elicit some assurance that in the meanwhile Peter would not place them in any other hands. Peter, at this, gave a laugh of harsher cadence than he intended, asking, justly enough, on what privilege his visitor rested such a demand and why he himself was disqualified from offering his wares to the highest bidder. "Surely you wouldn't hawk such things about?" cried Mr. Locket; but before Baron had time to retort cynically he added: "I'll publish your little story."

59

"Oh, thank you!"

"I'll publish anything you'll send me," Mr. Locket continued, as he went out. Peter had before this virtually given his word that for the letters he would treat only with the Promiscuous.

The young man passed, during a portion of the rest of the day, the strangest hours of his life. Yet he thought of them afterwards not as a phase of temptation, though they had been full of the emotion that accompanies an intense vision of alternatives. The struggle was already over; it seemed to him that, poor as he was, he was not poor enough to take Mr. Locket's money. He looked at the opposed courses with the self-possession of a man who has chosen, but this self-possession was in itself the most exquisite of excitements. It was really a high revulsion and a sort of noble pity. He seemed indeed to have his finger upon the pulse of history and to be in the secret of the gods. He had them all in his hand, the tablets and the scales and the torch. He couldn't keep a character together, but he might easily pull one to pieces. That would be "creative work" of a kind—he could reconstruct the character less pleasingly, could show an unknown side of it. Mr. Locket had had a good deal to say about responsibility; and responsibility in truth sat there with him all the morning, while he revolved in his narrow cage and, watching the crude spring rain on the windows, thought of the dismalness to which, at Dover, Mrs. Ryves was going back. This influence took in fact the form, put on the physiognomy of poor Sir Dominick Ferrand; he was at present as perceptible in it, as coldly and strangely personal, as if he had been a haunting ghost and had risen beside his own old hearthstone. Our friend was accustomed to his company and indeed had spent so many hours in it of late, following him up at the museum and comparing his different portraits, engravings and lithographs, in which there seemed to be conscious, pleading eyes for the betrayer, that their queer intimacy had grown as close as an embrace. Sir Dominick was very dumb, but he was terrible in his dependence, and Peter would not have encouraged him by so much curiosity nor reassured him by so much deference had it not been for the young man's complete acceptance of the impossibility of getting out of a tight place by exposing an individual. It didn't matter that the individual was dead; it didn't matter that he was dishonest. Peter felt him sufficiently alive to suffer; he perceived the rectification of history so conscientiously desired by Mr. Locket to be somehow for himself not an imperative task. It had come over him too definitely that in a case where one's success was to hinge upon an act of extradition it would minister most to an easy conscience to let the success go. No, no—even should he be starving he couldn't make money out of Sir Dominick's disgrace. He was almost surprised at the violence of the horror with which, as he shuffled mournfully about, the idea of any such profit inspired him. What was Sir Dominick to him after all? He wished he had never come across him.

In one of his brooding pauses at the window—the window out of which never again apparently should he see Mrs. Ryves glide across the little garden with the step for which he had liked her from the first—he became aware that the rain was about to intermit and the sun to make some grudging amends. This was a sign that he might go out; he had a vague perception that there were things to be done. He had work to look for, and a cheaper lodging, and a new idea (every idea he had ever cherished had left him), in addition to which the promised little word was to be dropped at Mr. Locket's door. He looked at his watch and was surprised at the hour, for he had nothing but a heartache to show for so much time. He would have to dress quickly, but as he passed to his bedroom his eye was caught by the little pyramid of letters which Mr. Locket had constructed on his davenport. They startled him and, staring at them, he stopped for an instant, half-amused, half-annoyed at their being still in existence. He had so completely destroyed them in spirit that he had taken the act for granted, and he was now reminded of the orderly stages of which an intention must consist to be sincere. Baron went at the papers with all his sincerity, and at his empty grate (where there lately had been no fire and he had only to remove a horrible ornament of tissue-paper dear to Mrs. Bundy) he burned the collection with infinite method. It made him feel happier to watch the worst pages turn to illegible ashes—if happiness be the right word to apply to his sense, in the process, of something so crisp and crackling that it suggested the death-rustle of bank-notes.

When ten minutes later he came back into his sitting-room, he seemed to himself oddly, unexpectedly in the presence of a bigger view. It was as if some interfering mass had been so displaced that he could see more sky and more country. Yet the opposite houses were naturally still there, and if the grimy little place looked lighter it was doubtless only because the rain had indeed stopped and the sun was pouring in. Peter went to the window to open it to the altered air, and in doing so beheld at the garden gate the humble "growler" in which a few hours before he had seen Mrs. Ryves take her departure. It was unmistakable—he remembered the knock-kneed white horse; but this made the fact that his friend's luggage no longer surmounted it only the more mystifying. Perhaps the cabman had already removed the luggage—he was now on his box smoking the short pipe that derived relish from inaction paid for. As Peter turned into the room again his ears caught a knock at his own door, a knock explained, as soon as he had responded, by the hard breathing of Mrs. Bundy.

"Please, sir, it's to say she've come back."

"What has she come back for?" Baron's question sounded ungracious, but his heartache had given another throb, and he felt a dread of another wound. It was like a practical joke.

"I think it's for you, sir," said Mrs. Bundy. "She'll see you for a moment, if you'll be so good, in the old place."

Peter followed his hostess downstairs, and Mrs. Bundy ushered him, with her company flourish, into the apartment she had fondly designated.

"I went away this morning, and I've only returned for an instant," said Mrs. Ryves, as soon as Mrs. Bundy had closed the door. He saw that she was different now; something had happened that had made her indulgent.

"Have you been all the way to Dover and back?"

"No, but I've been to Victoria. I've left my luggage there—I've been driving about."

"I hope you've enjoyed it."

"Very much. I've been to see Mr. Morrish."

"Mr. Morrish?"

"The musical publisher. I showed him our song. I played it for him, and he's delighted with it. He declares it's just the thing. He has given me fifty pounds. I think he believes in us," Mrs. Ryves went on, while Baron stared at the wonder—too sweet to be safe, it seemed to him as yet—of her standing there again before him and speaking of what they had in common. "Fifty pounds! fifty pounds!" she exclaimed, fluttering at him her happy cheque. She had come back, the first thing, to tell him, and of course his share of the money would be the half. She was rosy, jubilant, natural, she chattered like a happy woman. She said they must do more, ever so much more. Mr. Morrish had practically promised he would take anything that was as good as that. She had kept her cab because she was going to Dover; she couldn't leave the others alone. It was a vehicle infirm and inert, but Baron, after a little, appreciated its pace, for she had consented to his getting in with her and driving, this time in earnest, to Victoria. She had only come to tell him the good news—she repeated this assurance more than once. They talked of it so profoundly that it drove everything else for the time out of his head—his duty to Mr. Locket, the remarkable sacrifice he had just achieved, and even the odd coincidence, matching with the oddity of all the others, of her having reverted to the house again, as if with one of her famous divinations, at the very moment the trumpery papers, the origin really of their intimacy, had ceased to exist. But she, on her side, also had evidently forgotten the trumpery papers: she never mentioned them again, and Peter Baron never boasted of what he had done with them. He was silent for a while, from curiosity to see if her fine nerves had really given her a hint; and then later, when it came to be a question of his permanent attitude, he was silent, prodigiously, religiously, tremulously silent, in consequence of an extraordinary conversation that he had with her.

This conversation took place at Dover, when he went down to give her the money for which, at Mr. Morrish's bank, he had exchanged the cheque she had left with him. That cheque, or rather certain things it represented, had made somehow all the difference in their relations. The difference was huge, and Baron could think of nothing but this confirmed vision of their being able to work fruitfully together that would account for so rapid a change. She didn't talk of impossibilities now—she didn't seem to want to stop him off; only when, the day following his arrival at Dover with the fifty pounds (he had after all to agree to share them with her—he couldn't expect her to take a present of money from him), he returned to the question over which they had had their little scene the night they dined together—on this occasion (he had brought a portmanteau and he was staying) she mentioned that there was something very particular she had it on her conscience to tell him before letting him commit himself. There dawned in her face as she approached the subject a light of warning that frightened him; it was charged with something so strange that for an instant he held his breath. This flash of ugly possibilities passed however, and it was with the gesture of taking still tenderer possession of her, checked indeed by the grave, important way she held up a finger, that he answered: "Tell me everything—tell me!"

"You must know what I am—who I am; you must know especially what I'm not! There's a name for it, a hideous, cruel name. It's not my fault! Others have known, I've had to speak of it—it has made a great difference in my life. Surely you must have guessed!" she went on, with the thinnest quaver of irony, letting him now take her hand, which felt as cold as her hard duty. "Don't you see I've no belongings, no relations, no friends, nothing at all, in all the world, of my own? I was only a poor girl."

"A poor girl?" Baron was mystified, touched, distressed, piecing dimly together what she meant, but feeling, in a great surge of pity, that it was only something more to love her for.

"My mother—my poor mother," said Mrs. Ryves.

She paused with this, and through gathering tears her eyes met his as if to plead with him to understand. He understood, and drew her closer, but she kept herself free still, to continue: "She was a poor girl—she was only a governess; she was alone, she thought he loved her. He did—I think it was the only happiness she ever knew. But she died of it."

"Oh, I'm so glad you tell me—it's so grand of you!" Baron murmured. "Then—your father?" He hesitated, as if with his hands on old wounds.

64

"He had his own troubles, but he was kind to her. It was all misery and folly—he was married. He wasn't happy—there were good reasons, I believe, for that. I know it from letters, I know it from a person who's dead. Everyone is dead now—it's too far off. That's the only good thing. He was very kind to me; I remember him, though I didn't know then, as a little girl, who he was. He put me with some very good people—he did what he could for me. I think, later, his wife knew—a lady who came to see me once after his death. I was a very little girl, but I remember many things. What he could he did—something that helped me afterwards, something that helps me now. I think of him with a strange pity—I *see* him!" said Mrs. Ryves, with the faint past in her eyes. "You mustn't say anything against him," she added, gently and gravely.

"Never—never; for he has only made it more of a rapture to care for you."

"You must wait, you must think; we must wait together," she went on. "You can't tell, and you must give me time. Now that you know, it's all right; but you had to know. Doesn't it make us better friends?" asked Mrs. Ryves, with a tired smile which had the effect of putting the whole story further and further away. The next moment, however, she added quickly, as if with the sense that it couldn't be far enough: "You don't know, you can't judge, you must let it settle. Think of it, think of it; oh you will, and leave it so. I must have time myself, oh I must! Yes, you must believe me."

She turned away from him, and he remained looking at her a moment. "Ah, how I shall work for you!" he exclaimed.

"You must work for yourself; I'll help you." Her eyes had met his eyes again, and she added, hesitating, thinking: "You had better know, perhaps, who he was."

Baron shook his head, smiling confidently. "I don't care a straw."

"I do—a little. He was a great man."

"There must indeed have been some good in him."

"He was a high celebrity. You've often heard of him."

Baron wondered an instant. "I've no doubt you're a princess!" he said with a laugh. She made him nervous.

"I'm not ashamed of him. He was Sir Dominick Ferrand."

Baron saw in her face, in a few seconds, that she had seen something in his. He knew that he stared, then turned pale; it had the effect of a powerful shock. He was cold for an instant, as he had just found her, with the sense of danger, the confused horror of having dealt a blow. But the blood rushed back to its courses with his still quicker consciousness of safety, and he could make out, as he recovered his balance, that his emotion struck her simply as a violent surprise. He gave a muffled murmur: "Ah, it's you, my beloved!" which lost itself as he drew her close and held her long, in the intensity of his embrace and the wonder of his escape. It took more than a minute for him to say over to himself often enough, with his hidden face: "Ah, she must never, never know!"

She never knew; she only learned, when she asked him casually, that he had in fact destroyed the old documents she had had such a comic caprice about. The sensibility, the curiosity they had had the queer privilege of exciting in her had lapsed with the event as irresponsibly as they had arisen, and she appeared to have forgotten, or rather to attribute now to other causes, the agitation and several of the odd incidents that accompanied them. They naturally gave Peter Baron rather more to think about, much food, indeed, for clandestine meditation, some of which, in spite of the pains he took not to be caught, was noted by his friend and interpreted, to his knowledge, as depression produced by the long probation she succeeded in imposing on him. He was more patient than she could guess, with all her guessing, for if he was put to the proof she herself was not left undissected. It came back to him again and again that if the documents he had burned proved anything they proved that Sir Dominick Ferrand's human errors were not all of one order. The woman he loved was the daughter of her father, he couldn't get over that. What was more to the point was that as he came to know her better and better—for they did work together under Mr. Morrish's protection—his affection was a quantity still less to be neglected. He sometimes wondered, in the light of her general straightness (their marriage had brought out even more than he believed there was of it) whether the relics in the davenport were genuine. That piece of furniture is still almost as useful to him as Mr. Morrish's patronage. There is a tremendous run, as this gentlemen calls it, on several of their songs. Baron nevertheless still tries his hand also at prose, and his offerings are now not always declined by the magazines. But he has never approached the Promiscuous again. This periodical published in due course a highly eulogistic study of the remarkable career of Sir Dominick Ferrand.

About Author

Henry James OM (15 April 1843 – 28 February 1916) was an American-British author regarded as a key transitional figure between literary realism and literary modernism, and is considered by many to be among the greatest novelists in the English language. He was the son of Henry James Sr. and the brother of renowned philosopher and psychologist William James and diarist Alice James.

He is best known for a number of novels dealing with the social and marital interplay between émigré Americans, English people, and continental Europeans. Examples of such novels include The Portrait of a Lady, The Ambassadors, and The Wings of the Dove. His later works were increasingly experimental. In describing the internal states of mind and social dynamics of his characters, James often made use of a style in which ambiguous or contradictory motives and impressions were overlaid or juxtaposed in the discussion of a character's psyche. For their unique ambiguity, as well as for other aspects of their composition, his late works have been compared to impressionist painting.

His novella The Turn of the Screw has garnered a reputation as the most analysed and ambiguous ghost story in the English language and remains his most widely adapted work in other media. He also wrote a number of other highly regarded ghost stories and is considered one of the greatest masters of the field.

James published articles and books of criticism, travel, biography, autobiography, and plays. Born in the United States, James largely relocated to Europe as a young man and eventually settled in England, becoming a British subject in 1915, one year before his death. James was nominated for the Nobel Prize in Literature in 1911, 1912 and 1916.

Life

Early years, 1843–1883

James was born at 2 Washington Place in New York City on 15 April 1843. His parents were Mary Walsh and Henry James Sr. His father was intelligent and steadfastly congenial. He was a lecturer and philosopher who had inherited independent means from his father, an Albany banker and investor. Mary came from a wealthy family long settled in New York City. Her sister Katherine lived with her adult family for an extended period of time. Henry Jr. had three brothers, William, who was one year his senior, and younger brothers Wilkinson (Wilkie) and Robertson. His younger sister was Alice. Both of his parents were of Irish and Scottish descent.

The family first lived in Albany, at 70 N. Pearl St., and then moved to Fourteenth Street in New York City when James was still a young boy. His education was calculated by his father to expose him to many influences, primarily scientific and philosophical; it was described by Percy Lubbock, the editor of his selected letters, as "extraordinarily haphazard and promiscuous." James did not share the usual education in Latin and Greek classics. Between 1855 and 1860, the James' household traveled to London, Paris, Geneva, Boulogne-sur-Mer and Newport, Rhode Island, according to the father's current interests and publishing ventures, retreating to the United States when funds were low. Henry studied primarily with tutors and briefly attended schools while the family traveled in Europe. Their longest stays were in France, where Henry began to feel at home and became fluent in French. He was afflicted with a stutter, which seems to have manifested itself only when he spoke English; in French, he did not stutter.

In 1860 the family returned to Newport. There Henry became a friend of the painter John La Farge, who introduced him to French literature, and in particular, to Balzac. James later called Balzac his "greatest master," and said that he had learned more about the craft of fiction from him than from anyone else.

In the autumn of 1861 Henry received an injury, probably to his back, while fighting a fire. This injury, which resurfaced at times throughout his life, made him unfit for military service in the American Civil War.

In 1864 the James family moved to Boston, Massachusetts to be near William, who had enrolled first in the Lawrence Scientific School at Harvard and then in the medical school. In 1862 Henry attended Harvard Law School, but realised that he was not interested in studying law. He pursued his interest in literature and associated with authors and critics William Dean Howells and Charles Eliot Norton in Boston and Cambridge, formed lifelong friendships with Oliver Wendell Holmes Jr., the future Supreme Court Justice, and with James and Annie Fields, his first professional mentors.

His first published work was a review of a stage performance, "Miss Maggie Mitchell in Fanchon the Cricket," published in 1863. About a year later, A Tragedy of Error, his first short story, was published anonymously. James's first payment was for an appreciation of Sir Walter Scott's novels, written for the North American Review. He wrote fiction and non-fiction pieces for The Nation and Atlantic Monthly, where Fields was editor. In 1871 he published his first novel, Watch and Ward, in serial form in the Atlantic Monthly. The novel was later published in book form in 1878.

During a 14-month trip through Europe in 1869–70 he met Ruskin, Dickens, Matthew Arnold, William Morris, and George Eliot. Rome impressed him profoundly. "Here I am then in the Eternal City," he wrote to his brother William. "At last—for the first time—I live!" He attempted to support himself as a freelance writer in Rome, then secured a position as Paris correspondent for the New York Tribune, through the influence of its editor John Hay. When these efforts failed he returned to New York City. During 1874 and 1875 he published Transatlantic Sketches, A Passionate Pilgrim, and Roderick Hudson. During this early period in his career he was influenced by Nathaniel Hawthorne.

In 1869 he settled in London. There he established relationships with Macmillan and other publishers, who paid for serial installments that they would later publish in book form. The audience for these serialized novels was largely made up of middle-class women, and James struggled to fashion serious literary work within the strictures imposed by editors' and publishers' notions of what was suitable for young women to read. He lived in rented rooms but was able to join gentlemen's clubs that had libraries and where he could entertain male friends. He was introduced to English society by Henry Adams and Charles Milnes Gaskell, the latter introducing him to the Travellers' and the Reform Clubs.

In the fall of 1875 he moved to the Latin Quarter of Paris. Aside from two trips to America, he spent the next three decades—the rest of his life—in Europe. In Paris he met Zola, Alphonse Daudet, Maupassant, Turgenev, and others. He stayed in Paris only a year before moving to London.

In England he met the leading figures of politics and culture. He continued to be a prolific writer, producing The American (1877), The Europeans (1878), a revision of Watch and Ward (1878), French Poets and Novelists (1878), Hawthorne (1879), and several shorter works of fiction. In 1878 Daisy Miller established his fame on both sides of the Atlantic. It drew notice perhaps mostly because it depicted a woman whose behavior is outside the social norms of Europe. He also began his first masterpiece, The Portrait of a Lady, which would appear in 1881.

In 1877 he first visited Wenlock Abbey in Shropshire, home of his friend Charles Milnes Gaskell whom he had met through Henry Adams. He was much inspired by the darkly romantic Abbey and the surrounding countryside, which features in his essay Abbeys and Castles. In particular the gloomy monastic fishponds behind the Abbey are said to have inspired the lake in The Turn of the Screw.

While living in London, James continued to follow the careers of the "French realists", Émile Zola in particular. Their stylistic methods influenced his own work in the years to come. Hawthorne's influence on him faded during this period, replaced by George Eliot and Ivan Turgenev. 1879–1882 saw the publication of The Europeans, Washington Square, Confidence, and The Portrait of a Lady. He visited America in 1882–1883, then returned to London.

The period from 1881 to 1883 was marked by several losses. His mother died in 1881, followed by his father a few months later, and then by his brother Wilkie. Emerson, an old family friend, died in 1882. His friend Turgenev died in 1883.

Middle years, 1884–1897

In 1884 James made another visit to Paris. There he met again with Zola, Daudet, and Goncourt. He had been following the careers of the French "realist" or "naturalist" writers, and was increasingly influenced by them. In 1886, he published The Bostonians and The Princess Casamassima, both influenced by the French writers he'd studied assiduously. Critical reaction and sales were poor. He wrote to Howells that the books had hurt his career rather than helped because they had "reduced the desire, and demand, for my productions to zero". During this time he became friends with Robert Louis Stevenson, John Singer Sargent, Edmund Gosse, George du Maurier, Paul Bourget, and Constance Fenimore Woolson. His third novel from the 1880s was The Tragic Muse. Although he was following the precepts of Zola in his novels of the '80s, their tone and attitude are closer to the fiction of Alphonse Daudet. The lack of critical and financial success for his novels during this period led him to try writing for the theatre. (His dramatic works and his experiences with theatre are discussed below.)

In the last quarter of 1889, he started translating "for pure and copious lucre" Port Tarascon, the third volume of Alphonse Daudet adventures of Tartarin de Tarascon. Serialized in Harper's Monthly Magazine from June 1890, this translation praised as "clever" by The Spectator was published in January 1891 by Sampson Low, Marston, Searle & Rivington.

After the stage failure of Guy Domville in 1895, James was near despair and thoughts of death plagued him. The years spent on dramatic works were not entirely a loss. As he moved into the last phase of his career he found ways to adapt dramatic techniques into the novel form.

In the late 1880s and throughout the 1890s James made several trips through Europe. He spent a long stay in Italy in 1887. In that year the short novel The Aspern Papers and The Reverberator were published.

Late years, 1898–1916

In 1897–1898 he moved to Rye, Sussex, and wrote The Turn of the Screw. 1899–1900 saw the publication of The Awkward Age and The Sacred

Fount. During 1902–1904 he wrote The Ambassadors, The Wings of the Dove, and The Golden Bowl.

In 1904 he revisited America and lectured on Balzac. In 1906–1910 he published The American Scene and edited the "New York Edition", a 24-volume collection of his works. In 1910 his brother William died; Henry had just joined William from an unsuccessful search for relief in Europe on what then turned out to be his (Henry's) last visit to the United States (from summer 1910 to July 1911), and was near him, according to a letter he wrote, when he died.

In 1913 he wrote his autobiographies, A Small Boy and Others, and Notes of a Son and Brother. After the outbreak of the First World War in 1914 he did war work. In 1915 he became a British subject and was awarded the Order of Merit the following year. He died on 28 February 1916, in Chelsea, London. As he requested, his ashes were buried in Cambridge Cemetery in Massachusetts.

Biographers

James regularly rejected suggestions that he should marry, and after settling in London proclaimed himself "a bachelor". F. W. Dupee, in several volumes on the James family, originated the theory that he had been in love with his cousin Mary ("Minnie") Temple, but that a neurotic fear of sex kept him from admitting such affections: "James's invalidism ... was itself the symptom of some fear of or scruple against sexual love on his part." Dupee used an episode from James's memoir A Small Boy and Others, recounting a dream of a Napoleonic image in the Louvre, to exemplify James's romanticism about Europe, a Napoleonic fantasy into which he fled.

Dupee had not had access to the James family papers and worked principally from James's published memoir of his older brother, William, and the limited collection of letters edited by Percy Lubbock, heavily weighted toward James's last years. His account therefore moved directly from James's childhood, when he trailed after his older brother, to elderly invalidism. As more material became available to scholars, including the diaries of contemporaries and hundreds of affectionate and sometimes erotic letters written by James to younger men, the picture of neurotic celibacy gave way to a portrait of a closeted homosexual.

Between 1953 and 1972, Leon Edel authored a major five-volume biography of James, which accessed unpublished letters and documents after Edel gained the permission of James's family. Edel's portrayal of James included the suggestion he was celibate. It was a view first propounded by critic Saul Rosenzweig in 1943. In 1996 Sheldon M. Novick published Henry James: The Young Master, followed by Henry James: The Mature Master (2007). The first book "caused something of an uproar in Jamesian circles" as it challenged the previous received notion of celibacy, a once-familiar paradigm in biographies of homosexuals when direct evidence was non-existent. Novick also criticised Edel for following the discounted Freudian interpretation of homosexuality "as a kind of failure." The difference of opinion erupted in a series of exchanges between Edel and Novick which were published by the online magazine Slate, with the latter arguing that even the suggestion of celibacy went against James's own injunction "live!"—not "fantasize!"

A letter James wrote in old age to Hugh Walpole has been cited as an explicit statement of this. Walpole confessed to him of indulging in "high jinks", and James wrote a reply endorsing it: "We must know, as much as possible, in our beautiful art, yours & mine, what we are talking about — & the only way to know it is to have lived & loved & cursed & floundered & enjoyed & suffered — I don't think I regret a single 'excess' of my responsive youth".

The interpretation of James as living a less austere emotional life has been subsequently explored by other scholars. The often intense politics of Jamesian scholarship has also been the subject of studies. Author Colm Tóibín has said that Eve Kosofsky Sedgwick's Epistemology of the Closet made a landmark difference to Jamesian scholarship by arguing that he be read as a homosexual writer whose desire to keep his sexuality a secret shaped his layered style and dramatic artistry. According to Tóibín such a reading "removed James from the realm of dead white males who wrote about posh people. He became our contemporary."

James's letters to expatriate American sculptor Hendrik Christian Andersen have attracted particular attention. James met the 27-year-old Andersen in Rome in 1899, when James was 56, and wrote letters to Andersen that are intensely emotional: "I hold you, dearest boy, in my innermost love, & count on your feeling me—in every throb of your soul". In a letter of 6 May 1904, to his brother William, James referred to himself as "always your hopelessly celibate even though sexagenarian Henry". How accurate that description might have been is the subject of contention among James's biographers, but the letters to Andersen were occasionally quasi-erotic: "I put, my dear boy, my arm around you, & feel the pulsation, thereby, as it were, of our excellent future & your admirable endowment." To his homosexual friend Howard Sturgis, James could write: "I repeat, almost to indiscretion, that I could live with you. Meanwhile I can only try to live without you."

His numerous letters to the many young gay men among his close male friends are more forthcoming. In a letter to Howard Sturgis, following a long visit, James refers jocularly to their "happy little congress of two" and in letters to Hugh Walpole he pursues convoluted jokes and puns about their relationship, referring to himself as an elephant who "paws you oh so benevolently" and winds about Walpole his "well meaning old trunk". His letters to Walter Berry printed by the Black Sun Press have long been celebrated for their lightly veiled eroticism.

He corresponded in almost equally extravagant language with his many female friends, writing, for example, to fellow novelist Lucy Clifford: "Dearest Lucy! What shall I say? when I love you so very, very much, and see you nine times for once that I see Others! Therefore I think that—if you want it made clear to the meanest intelligence—I love you more than I love Others." To his New York friend Mary Cadwalader Jones: "Dearest Mary Cadwalader. I yearn over you, but I yearn in vain; & your long silence really breaks my heart, mystifies, depresses, almost alarms me, to the point even of making me wonder if poor unconscious & doting old Célimare [Jones's pet name for James] has 'done' anything, in some dark somnambulism of the spirit, which has ... given you a bad moment, or a wrong impression, or a 'colourable pretext' ... However these things may be, he loves you as tenderly as ever;

nothing, to the end of time, will ever detach him from you, & he remembers those Eleventh St. matutinal intimes hours, those telephonic matinées, as the most romantic of his life ..." His long friendship with American novelist Constance Fenimore Woolson, in whose house he lived for a number of weeks in Italy in 1887, and his shock and grief over her suicide in 1894, are discussed in detail in Edel's biography and play a central role in a study by Lyndall Gordon. (Edel conjectured that Woolson was in love with James and killed herself in part because of his coldness, but Woolson's biographers have objected to Edel's account.)

Works

Style and themes

James is one of the major figures of trans-Atlantic literature. His works frequently juxtapose characters from the Old World (Europe), embodying a feudal civilisation that is beautiful, often corrupt, and alluring, and from the New World (United States), where people are often brash, open, and assertive and embody the virtues—freedom and a more highly evolved moral character—of the new American society. James explores this clash of personalities and cultures, in stories of personal relationships in which power is exercised well or badly. His protagonists were often young American women facing oppression or abuse, and as his secretary Theodora Bosanquet remarked in her monograph Henry James at Work:

> When he walked out of the refuge of his study and into the world and looked around him, he saw a place of torment, where creatures of prey perpetually thrust their claws into the quivering flesh of doomed, defenseless children of light ... His novels are a repeated exposure of this wickedness, a reiterated and passionate plea for the fullest freedom of development, unimperiled by reckless and barbarous stupidity.

Critics have jokingly described three phases in the development of James's prose: "James I, James II, and The Old Pretender." He wrote short stories and plays. Finally, in his third and last period he returned to the long, serialised novel. Beginning in the second period, but most noticeably in the third, he increasingly abandoned direct statement in favour of frequent double negatives, and complex descriptive imagery. Single paragraphs began to run for page after page, in which an initial noun would be succeeded by pronouns surrounded by clouds of adjectives and prepositional clauses, far from their original referents, and verbs would be deferred and then preceded by a series of adverbs. The overall effect could be a vivid evocation of a scene as perceived by a sensitive observer. It has been debated whether this change of style was engendered by James's shifting from writing to dictating to a typist, a change made during the composition of What Maisie Knew.

In its intense focus on the consciousness of his major characters, James's later work foreshadows extensive developments in 20th century fiction. Indeed, he might have influenced stream-of-consciousness writers such as Virginia Woolf, who not only read some of his novels but also wrote essays about them. Both contemporary and modern readers have found the late style difficult and unnecessary; his friend Edith Wharton, who admired him greatly, said that there were passages in his work that were all but incomprehensible. James was harshly portrayed by H. G. Wells as a hippopotamus laboriously attempting to pick up a pea that had got into a corner of its cage. The "late James" style was ably parodied by Max Beerbohm in "The Mote in the Middle Distance".

More important for his work overall may have been his position as an expatriate, and in other ways an outsider, living in Europe. While he came from middle-class and provincial beginnings (seen from the perspective of European polite society) he worked very hard to gain access to all levels of society, and the settings of his fiction range from working class to aristocratic, and often describe the efforts of middle-class Americans to make their way in European capitals. He confessed he got some of his best story ideas from gossip at the dinner table or at country house weekends. He worked for a living, however, and lacked the experiences of select schools, university, and army service, the common bonds of masculine society. He was furthermore a man whose tastes and interests were, according to the prevailing standards of Victorian era Anglo-American culture, rather feminine, and who was shadowed by the cloud of prejudice that then and later accompanied suspicions of his homosexuality. Edmund Wilson famously compared James's objectivity to Shakespeare's:

One would be in a position to appreciate James better if one compared him with the dramatists of the seventeenth century—Racine and Molière, whom he resembles in form as well as in point of view, and even Shakespeare, when allowances are made for the most extreme differences in subject and form. These poets are not, like Dickens and Hardy, writers of melodrama—either humorous or pessimistic, nor secretaries of society like Balzac, nor prophets like Tolstoy: they are occupied simply with the presentation of conflicts of moral character, which they do not concern themselves about softening or averting. They do not indict society for these situations: they regard them as universal and inevitable. They do not even blame God for allowing them: they accept them as the conditions of life.

It is also possible to see many of James's stories as psychological thought-experiments. In his preface to the New York edition of The American he describes the development of the story in his mind as exactly such: the "situation" of an American, "some robust but insidiously beguiled and betrayed, some cruelly wronged, compatriot..." with the focus of the story being on the response of this wronged man. The Portrait of a Lady may be an experiment to see what happens when an idealistic young woman suddenly becomes very rich. In many of his tales, characters seem to exemplify alternative futures and possibilities, as most markedly in "The Jolly Corner", in which the protagonist and a ghost-doppelganger live alternative American and European lives; and in others, like The Ambassadors, an older James seems fondly to regard his own younger self facing a crucial moment.

Major novels

The first period of James's fiction, usually considered to have culminated in The Portrait of a Lady, concentrated on the contrast between Europe and America. The style of these novels is generally straightforward and, though personally characteristic, well within the norms of 19th-century fiction. Roderick Hudson (1875) is a Künstlerroman that traces the development of the title character, an extremely talented sculptor. Although the book shows some signs of immaturity—this was James's first serious attempt at a full-length novel—it has attracted favourable comment due to the vivid realisation of the three major characters: Roderick Hudson, superbly gifted but unstable and unreliable; Rowland Mallet, Roderick's limited but much more mature friend and patron; and Christina Light, one of James's most enchanting and maddening femmes fatales. The pair of Hudson and Mallet has been seen as representing the two sides of James's own nature: the wildly imaginative artist and the brooding conscientious mentor.

In The Portrait of a Lady (1881) James concluded the first phase of his career with a novel that remains his most popular piece of long fiction. The story is of a spirited young American woman, Isabel Archer, who "affronts her destiny" and finds it overwhelming. She inherits a large amount of money and subsequently becomes the victim of Machiavellian scheming by two American expatriates. The narrative is set mainly in Europe, especially in England and Italy. Generally regarded as the masterpiece of his early phase, The Portrait of a Lady is described as a psychological novel, exploring the minds of his characters, and almost a work of social science, exploring the differences between Europeans and Americans, the old and the new worlds.

The second period of James's career, which extends from the publication of The Portrait of a Lady through the end of the nineteenth century, features less popular novels including The Princess Casamassima, published serially in The Atlantic Monthly in 1885–1886, and The Bostonians, published serially in The Century Magazine during the same period. This period also featured James's celebrated Gothic novella, The Turn of the Screw.

The third period of James's career reached its most significant achievement in three novels published just around the start of the 20th century: The Wings of the Dove (1902), The Ambassadors (1903), and The Golden Bowl (1904). Critic F. O. Matthiessen called this "trilogy" James's major phase, and these novels have certainly received intense critical study. It was the second-written of the books, The Wings of the Dove (1902) that was the first published because it attracted no serialization. This novel tells the story of Milly Theale, an American heiress stricken with a serious disease, and her impact on the people around her. Some of these people befriend Milly with honourable motives, while others are more self-interested. James stated in his autobiographical books that Milly was based on Minny Temple, his beloved cousin who died at an early age of tuberculosis. He said that he attempted in the novel to wrap her memory in the "beauty and dignity of art".

Shorter narratives

James was particularly interested in what he called the "beautiful and blest nouvelle", or the longer form of short narrative. Still, he produced a number of very short stories in which he achieved notable compression of sometimes complex subjects. The following narratives are representative of James's achievement in the shorter forms of fiction.

- "A Tragedy of Error" (1864), short story
- "The Story of a Year" (1865), short story
- A Passionate Pilgrim (1871), novella
- Madame de Mauves (1874), novella
- Daisy Miller (1878), novella
- The Aspern Papers (1888), novella
- The Lesson of the Master (1888), novella
- The Pupil (1891), short story
- "The Figure in the Carpet" (1896), short story
- The Beast in the Jungle (1903), novella
- An International Episode (1878)
- Picture and Text
- Four Meetings (1885)
- A London Life, and Other Tales (1889)
- The Spoils of Poynton (1896)

- Embarrassments (1896)

- The Two Magics: The Turn of the Screw, Covering End (1898)

- A Little Tour of France (1900)

- The Sacred Fount (1901)

- Views and Reviews (1908)

- The Wings of the Dove, Volume I (1902)

- The Wings of the Dove, Volume II (1909)

- The Finer Grain (1910)

- The Outcry (1911)

- Lady Barbarina: The Siege of London, An International Episode and Other Tales (1922)

- The Birthplace (1922)

Plays

At several points in his career James wrote plays, beginning with one-act plays written for periodicals in 1869 and 1871 and a dramatisation of his popular novella Daisy Miller in 1882. From 1890 to 1892, having received a bequest that freed him from magazine publication, he made a strenuous effort to succeed on the London stage, writing a half-dozen plays of which only one, a dramatisation of his novel The American, was produced. This play was performed for several years by a touring repertory company and had a respectable run in London, but did not earn very much money for James. His other plays written at this time were not produced.

In 1893, however, he responded to a request from actor-manager George Alexander for a serious play for the opening of his renovated St. James's Theatre, and wrote a long drama, Guy Domville, which Alexander produced. There was a noisy uproar on the opening night, 5 January 1895, with hissing from the gallery when James took his bow after the final curtain, and the author was upset. The play received moderately good reviews and had a modest run of four weeks before being taken off to make way for Oscar Wilde's The Importance of Being Earnest, which Alexander thought would have better prospects for the coming season.

After the stresses and disappointment of these efforts James insisted that he would write no more for the theatre, but within weeks had agreed to write a curtain-raiser for Ellen Terry. This became the one-act "Summersoft", which he later rewrote into a short story, "Covering End", and then expanded into a full-length play, The High Bid, which had a brief run in London in 1907, when James made another concerted effort to write for the stage. He wrote three new plays, two of which were in production when the death of Edward VII on 6 May 1910 plunged London into mourning and theatres closed. Discouraged by failing health and the stresses of theatrical work, James did not renew his efforts in the theatre, but recycled his plays as successful novels. The Outcry was a best-seller in the United States when it was published in 1911. During the years 1890–1893 when he was most engaged with the theatre, James wrote a good deal of theatrical criticism and assisted Elizabeth Robins and others in translating and producing Henrik Ibsen for the first time in London.

Leon Edel argued in his psychoanalytic biography that James was traumatised by the opening night uproar that greeted Guy Domville, and that it plunged him into a prolonged depression. The successful later novels, in Edel's view, were the result of a kind of self-analysis, expressed in fiction, which partly freed him from his fears. Other biographers and scholars have not accepted this account, however; the more common view being that of F.O. Matthiessen, who wrote: "Instead of being crushed by the collapse of his hopes [for the theatre]... he felt a resurgence of new energy."

Non-fiction

Beyond his fiction, James was one of the more important literary critics in the history of the novel. In his classic essay The Art of Fiction (1884), he argued against rigid prescriptions on the novelist's choice of subject and method of treatment. He maintained that the widest possible freedom in content and approach would help ensure narrative fiction's continued vitality.

James wrote many valuable critical articles on other novelists; typical is his book-length study of Nathaniel Hawthorne, which has been the subject of critical debate. Richard Brodhead has suggested that the study was emblematic of James's struggle with Hawthorne's influence, and constituted an effort to place the elder writer "at a disadvantage." Gordon Fraser, meanwhile, has suggested that the study was part of a more commercial effort by James to introduce himself to British readers as Hawthorne's natural successor.

When James assembled the New York Edition of his fiction in his final years, he wrote a series of prefaces that subjected his own work to searching, occasionally harsh criticism.

At 22 James wrote The Noble School of Fiction for The Nation's first issue in 1865. He would write, in all, over 200 essays and book, art, and theatre reviews for the magazine.

For most of his life James harboured ambitions for success as a playwright. He converted his novel The American into a play that enjoyed modest returns in the early 1890s. In all he wrote about a dozen plays, most of which went unproduced. His costume drama Guy Domville failed disastrously on its opening night in 1895. James then largely abandoned his efforts to conquer the stage and returned to his fiction. In his Notebooks he maintained that his theatrical experiment benefited his novels and tales by helping him dramatise his characters' thoughts and emotions. James produced a small but valuable amount of theatrical criticism, including perceptive appreciations of Henrik Ibsen.

With his wide-ranging artistic interests, James occasionally wrote on the visual arts. Perhaps his most valuable contribution was his favourable assessment of fellow expatriate John Singer Sargent, a painter whose critical status has improved markedly in recent decades. James also wrote sometimes charming, sometimes brooding articles about various places he visited and lived in. His most famous books of travel writing include Italian Hours (an example of the charming approach) and The American Scene (most definitely on the brooding side).

James was one of the great letter-writers of any era. More than ten thousand of his personal letters are extant, and over three thousand have been published in a large number of collections. A complete edition of James's letters began publication in 2006, edited by Pierre Walker and Greg Zacharias. As of 2014, eight volumes have been published, covering the period from 1855 to 1880. James's correspondents included celebrated contemporaries like Robert Louis Stevenson, Edith Wharton and Joseph Conrad, along with many others in his wide circle of friends and acquaintances. The letters range from the "mere twaddle of graciousness" to serious discussions of artistic, social and personal issues.

Very late in life James began a series of autobiographical works: A Small Boy and Others, Notes of a Son and Brother, and the unfinished The Middle Years. These books portray the development of a classic observer who was passionately interested in artistic creation but was somewhat reticent about participating fully in the life around him.

Reception

Criticism, biographies and fictional treatments

James's work has remained steadily popular with the limited audience of educated readers to whom he spoke during his lifetime, and has remained firmly in the canon, but, after his death, some American critics, such as Van Wyck Brooks, expressed hostility towards James for his long expatriation and eventual naturalisation as a British subject. Other critics such as E. M. Forster complained about what they saw as James's squeamishness in the treatment of sex and other possibly controversial material, or dismissed his late style as difficult and obscure, relying heavily on extremely long sentences and excessively latinate language. Similarly Oscar Wilde criticised him for writing "fiction as if it were a painful duty". Vernon Parrington, composing a canon of American literature, condemned James for having cut himself off from America. Jorge Luis Borges wrote about him, "Despite the scruples and delicate complexities of James, his work suffers from a major defect: the absence of life." And Virginia Woolf, writing to Lytton Strachey, asked, "Please tell me what you find in Henry James. ... we have his works here, and

I read, and I can't find anything but faintly tinged rose water, urbane and sleek, but vulgar and pale as Walter Lamb. Is there really any sense in it?" The novelist W. Somerset Maugham wrote, "He did not know the English as an Englishman instinctively knows them and so his English characters never to my mind quite ring true," and argued "The great novelists, even in seclusion, have lived life passionately. Henry James was content to observe it from a window." Maugham nevertheless wrote, "The fact remains that those last novels of his, notwithstanding their unreality, make all other novels, except the very best, unreadable." Colm Tóibín observed that James "never really wrote about the English very well. His English characters don't work for me."

Despite these criticisms, James is now valued for his psychological and moral realism, his masterful creation of character, his low-key but playful humour, and his assured command of the language. In his 1983 book, The Novels of Henry James, Edward Wagenknecht offers an assessment that echoes Theodora Bosanquet's:

> "To be completely great," Henry James wrote in an early review, "a work of art must lift up the heart," and his own novels do this to an outstanding degree ... More than sixty years after his death, the great novelist who sometimes professed to have no opinions stands foursquare in the great Christian humanistic and democratic tradition. The men and women who, at the height of World War II, raided the secondhand shops for his out-of-print books knew what they were about. For no writer ever raised a braver banner to which all who love freedom might adhere.

William Dean Howells saw James as a representative of a new realist school of literary art which broke with the English romantic tradition epitomised by the works of Charles Dickens and William Makepeace Thackeray. Howells wrote that realism found "its chief exemplar in Mr. James... A novelist he is not, after the old fashion, or after any fashion but his own." F.R. Leavis championed Henry James as a novelist of "established pre-eminence" in The Great Tradition (1948), asserting that The Portrait of a Lady and The Bostonians were "the two most brilliant novels in the language." James is now prized as a master of point of view who moved literary fiction forward by insisting in showing, not telling, his stories to the reader. (Source: Wikipedia)

NOTABLE WORKS

NOVELS

Watch and Ward (1871)

Roderick Hudson (1875)

The American (1877)

The Europeans (1878)

Confidence (1879)

Washington Square (1880)

The Portrait of a Lady (1881)

The Bostonians (1886)

The Princess Casamassima (1886)

The Reverberator (1888)

The Tragic Muse (1890)

The Other House (1896)

The Spoils of Poynton (1897)

What Maisie Knew (1897)

The Awkward Age (1899)

The Sacred Fount (1901)

The Wings of the Dove (1902)

The Ambassadors (1903)

The Golden Bowl (1904)

The Whole Family (collaborative novel with eleven other authors, 1908)

The Outcry (1911)

The Ivory Tower (unfinished, published posthumously 1917)

The Sense of the Past (unfinished, published posthumously 1917)

SHORT STORIES AND NOVELLAS

A Tragedy of Error (1864)

The Story of a Year (1865)

A Landscape Painter (1866)

A Day of Days (1866)

My Friend Bingham (1867)

Poor Richard (1867)

The Story of a Masterpiece (1868)

A Most Extraordinary Case (1868)

A Problem (1868)

De Grey: A Romance (1868)

Osborne's Revenge (1868)

The Romance of Certain Old Clothes (1868)

A Light Man (1869)

Gabrielle de Bergerac (1869)

Travelling Companions (1870)

A Passionate Pilgrim (1871)

At Isella (1871)

Master Eustace (1871)

Guest's Confession (1872)

The Madonna of the Future (1873)

The Sweetheart of M. Briseux (1873)

The Last of the Valerii (1874)

Madame de Mauves (1874)

Adina (1874)

Professor Fargo (1874)

Eugene Pickering (1874)

Benvolio (1875)

Crawford's Consistency (1876)

The Ghostly Rental (1876)

Four Meetings (1877)

Rose-Agathe (1878, as Théodolinde)

Daisy Miller (1878)

Longstaff's Marriage (1878)

An International Episode (1878)

The Pension Beaurepas (1879)

A Diary of a Man of Fifty (1879)

A Bundle of Letters (1879)

The Point of View (1882)

The Siege of London (1883)

Impressions of a Cousin (1883)

Lady Barberina (1884)

Pandora (1884)

The Author of Beltraffio (1884)

Georgina's Reasons (1884)

A New England Winter (1884)

The Path of Duty (1884)

Mrs. Temperly (1887)

Louisa Pallant (1888)

The Aspern Papers (1888)

The Liar (1888)

The Modern Warning (1888, originally published as The Two Countries)

A London Life (1888)

The Patagonia (1888)

The Lesson of the Master (1888)

The Solution (1888)

The Pupil (1891)

Brooksmith (1891)

The Marriages (1891)

The Chaperon (1891)

Sir Edmund Orme (1891)

Nona Vincent (1892)

The Real Thing (1892)

The Private Life (1892)

Lord Beaupré (1892)

The Visits (1892)

Sir Dominick Ferrand (1892)

Greville Fane (1892)

Collaboration (1892)

Owen Wingrave (1892)

The Wheel of Time (1892)

The Middle Years (1893)

The Death of the Lion (1894)

The Coxon Fund (1894)

The Next Time (1895)

Glasses (1896)

The Altar of the Dead (1895)

The Figure in the Carpet (1896)

The Way It Came (1896, also published as The Friends of the Friends)

The Turn of the Screw (1898)

Covering End (1898)

In the Cage (1898)

John Delavoy (1898)

The Given Case (1898)

Europe (1899)

The Great Condition (1899)

The Real Right Thing (1899)

Paste (1899)

The Great Good Place (1900)

Maud-Evelyn (1900)

Miss Gunton of Poughkeepsie (1900)

The Tree of Knowledge (1900)

The Abasement of the Northmores (1900)

The Third Person (1900)

The Special Type (1900)

The Tone of Time (1900)

Broken Wings (1900)

The Two Faces (1900)

Mrs. Medwin (1901)

The Beldonald Holbein (1901)

The Story in It (1902)

Flickerbridge (1902)

The Birthplace (1903)

The Beast in the Jungle (1903)

The Papers (1903)

Fordham Castle (1904)

Julia Bride (1908)

The Jolly Corner (1908)

The Velvet Glove (1909)

Mora Montravers (1909)

Crapy Cornelia (1909)

The Bench of Desolation (1909)

A Round of Visits (1910)

OTHER

Transatlantic Sketches (1875)

French Poets and Novelists (1878)

Hawthorne (1879)

Portraits of Places (1883)

A Little Tour in France (1884)

Partial Portraits (1888)

Essays in London and Elsewhere (1893)

Picture and Text (1893)

Terminations (1893)

Theatricals (1894)

Theatricals: Second Series (1895)

Guy Domville (1895)

The Soft Side (1900)

William Wetmore Story and His Friends (1903)

The Better Sort (1903)

English Hours (1905)

The Question of our Speech; The Lesson of Balzac. Two Lectures (1905)

The American Scene (1907)

Views and Reviews (1908)

Italian Hours (1909)

A Small Boy and Others (1913)

Notes on Novelists (1914)

Notes of a Son and Brother (1914)

Within the Rim (1918)

Travelling Companions (1919)

Notebooks (various, published posthumously)

The Middle Years (unfinished, published posthumously 1917)

A Most Unholy Trade (1925, published posthumously)

The Art of the Novel : Critical Prefaces (1934)